CIRCLE °F MAGIC

Daja's Book

BY TAM°RA PIERCE

SCHOLASTIC INC.

New York Toronto London Auckland Sydney
Mexico City New Delhi Hong Kong

POINT

ACKNOWLEDGMENTS

Thanks are due to my husband, Tim, for the help, encouragement
and advice that saw me through a most worrisome first draft;
to Rick Robinson once again for fast turnaround proofreading
and intelligent reader reaction; to my agent, Craig R. Tenney,
the personification of grace under fire; and to my editor,
Anne Dunn, who took time from her own hectic schedule to help
me get this book out the gate and who gave me leeway when it
came to handing in the first draft.
As always, thanks go to Thomas Gansevoort,
this series's creative godfather.

ISBN 0-590-55410-7

12 11 10 9 8 7 6 5 4   0 1 2 3 4 5/0

Printed in the U.S.A.   01

First Scholastic Trade paperback printing, March 2000

The display type is Sophia.
The text type is Berling Roman.

Map by Ian Schoenherr
Interior design by Cathy Bobak
Cover design by Ursula Albano
Cover painting by Theron

1

Sunset blazed above Gold Ridge Valley in north Emelan, throwing shadows over a company of mounted riders. At the head of their train a banner-man carried the personal flag of Duke Vedris IV, ruler of Emelan. The duke himself rode behind the flag, surrounded and followed by his staff, guards, and friends. Smoke drifted through the air in veils, stinging everyone's eyes. They had been riding through it for two days, watching it stretch over pastures and fields. Now at last, as the company entered the forests that filled the northern half of the valley, they began to rise above the thick air.

At the very rear of their column rode three girls

and a boy, all mounted on sturdy ponies. When one of the adults, a woman in a dark green habit, stopped and dismounted from her horse, they also drew their ponies to a halt and watched her. She climbed out of the sunken road and walked several yards under the ancient trees. A big dog with curly white fur who trotted beside the four detached himself from their group and followed.

"Little Bear!" called Daja Kisubo, a tall, broad-shouldered black girl. "Let Rosethorn alone. Come back here."

The dog Little Bear obeyed. When he reached the closest rider—Daja's plump, redheaded friend Tris—he sat, stirring the road's dust with his plumed tail.

"Rosethorn?" asked Briar, the boy. "Is everything all right?"

"Just stay put," ordered Rosethorn. She picked up a sturdy branch and began to dig in the heavy litter of tree leaves and decaying wood underfoot. "I'll be there in a moment."

"That's *not* what I asked," Briar muttered to the girls out of the corner of his mouth. "I *asked* if everything was all right."

Daja turned her mount. From this small rise she could look through a gap in the trees.

"Daja? Are *you* all right?" The voice belonged to the third girl in their party, Sandry. Everything about her, from her pony to her clothes, spoke of wealth that the other three young people did not have. When she turned her mount to see what had caught Daja's eye, Briar and Tris did the same.

In the distance, where ridges of open pasture faded into the base of the southern and western mountains, long bands of sullen orange fire shone. Daja shook her head, making her eleven short braids flap. "It's like something from a nightmare," she replied. "It looks like what the Traders call *pijule fakol.*"

Sandry shivered and drew the gods-circle on her chest for protection. She knew Trader beliefs. "The afterlife for those who don't pay their debts," she muttered.

Little Bear rose to his hind legs, planting his forepaws against Tris's saddle. She leaned over to scratch his ears, her brass-rimmed spectacles glinting in the late afternoon sun. "That's the nice thing about believing in the Living Circle," she remarked. "No bad afterlives. We just get reborn."

Briar squinted, his gray-green eyes wary. "Those fires reach for *miles*. And there's nothing to stop them from burning. This whole country's dry as tinder."

Rosethorn thrust a clump of tree-litter into a pocket, then returned to her mount. Once she was in the saddle, she beckoned to a local man who rode with the duke's party. "How long has it been since you people last had a forest fire?"

The man chuckled. "Bless you, Dedicate Rosethorn, there's not been what I'd call a *real* forest fire in this valley since—oh, since my dad was a pup. Our mage, him they call Firetamer, he tends to *all* our fires."

"I was afraid you'd say that," murmured Rosethorn, an earth dedicate of the Living Circle temples. "Come on, you four—we're being left behind."

Sandry urged her pony forward. Tris, Briar, and Little Bear fell in beside her.

Daja stayed where she was for a moment, her troubled dark eyes still on the blazes. How could anything as wonderful as fire look so menacing? she wondered. She worked with it every day; it was her friend. What if one day it turned against her as it had against Gold Ridge's fields?

"Stay in *pijule fakol*, where you belong," Daja Kisubo muttered to the distant flames. Clucking to her pony, she rode to catch up with her friends.

The next day Daja entered a small local smithy, loaded down with tools. She dropped everything beside the rough anvil, then realized that the staff she always carried had fallen to the ground as well. Swiftly she grabbed it from the pile, dusting its polished wood. She rested the staff against the wall near the hearth, stopping for a moment to run her fingers over its mirror-bright, unmarked brass cap. That bit of metalwork told those who knew how to read Trader staffs that she was *trangshi*, an outcast, with the worst luck in the world.

She turned her back on it and surveyed the cramped and dirty smithy. I wish I were *home*, she thought, eyeing the forge.

Home was the temple city of Winding Circle, where her master had a proper clean, well-lit forge. This dismal place was the twelfth smithy that she'd had to work in since the duke's train began its journey. She was alone; the smith—who was also the village headman—was talking with the duke about what was needed to help this tiny valley survive the winter.

The smith's absence, at least, was a good thing. Even his apprentice was gone, visiting a sick mother. She hated working in front of strangers. She was also tired of back country craftsmen who told her and her teacher Frostpine that they had things soft in Winding Circle. As if we did no real work of our own, she thought, inspecting the stone forge. Here was a pleasant surprise: the smith's apprentice must have cleaned out the nest-shaped firepit and laid kindling for a new fire. He'd left her that much less work.

Looking at the kindling, she reached deep inside her to find her magic. Drawing out just a touch, she blew it into the firepit. Flames sprang up instantly.

Next she sent her power outside through the wall, to the other end of the tube through which the outdoor bellows pumped air under the fire inside. Since that summer, when Sandry had made the four friends' magics into one, they had been able to talk in thought-form and to enter each other's minds if they needed to. The ability was quite useful, particularly when one of them needed something from the others. *Tri-is . . .* Daja mind-called.

I know, I know. The magic under Trisana Chandler's reply felt like cool winds and heavy mist. *I had to pull the bellows out of the opening. You might want to stand away from the fire.*

Not too much at first, Daja told her, then backed up. The burning heap of kindling fluttered, then blazed as air from the outside was thrust in under its flames. Daja heaped fresh charcoal around the sides of the kindling. Once it had caught, she added still more. *Now give me some real air,* she told her friend.

The answer came in the shape of a heavier stream of wind rushing through the opening under the forge. More charcoal caught. Daja stacked fuel until she had the right kind of fire to work her iron rods with.

Just keep it steady for now, she mind-called to her friend. *I hope you brought something to read.*

She felt Tris settle on a bench near the opening in the wall. Using one hand the other girl picked up a book. With the other she drew a skein of breeze from the sky into the bellows-hole.

It's A History of Volcanoes, Hot Springs, and Mud Pots in the Mountains of Emelan. *There's a lot of information in it,* Tris explained.

Sounds ravishing, Daja commented. Letting the magical conversation go, she grabbed a handful of long, thin iron rods, carried them over to the forge-fire, and put them in to heat.

She felt bad for Tris, stuck behind the forge. Her redheaded friend would have liked nothing better than to ride with the duke and their teachers, exploring the valley. Unfortunately, when Tris got cross, small winds turned to big ones. No one wanted her anywhere near the grassfires they had gone to inspect today.

Unlike Tris, Daja had no interest in grassfires and had said as much to her teacher Frostpine. She had *wanted* him to give her something new to work, like the ruddy copper that was mined in these parts. Instead he'd assigned her the most humdrum task an apprentice could get.

Nails, Daja thought tiredly. Barehanded, she drew a thin, cherry-red iron rod out of the fire. I dream of forging swords and crowns and armor, but what does he give me? Nails. She carried her rod over to the anvil and examined its gloryless surface.

The light in the small building was poor, the outer air smoky. The forge-fire itself was sinking to become a steady wash of heat over red coals, without giving much light. She would have to do something about that.

Daja reached a hand toward the forge and twitched her fingers. A rope of fire rose from the coals. A second finger-twitch brought the rope toward the anvil. She stopped it a foot away, then thought for a moment. Her plan was to shape it like a branch of candles, but something else nudged her, wanting to press its own image into the flame. She let it roll away from her and into the rope. It split, then split again, turning itself into a multitude of fibers. These began to weave themselves in and out of each other. When they halted, a grid of flame hung in the air, like a broadly woven square of cloth. Daja could have stuck a thumb into the gaps between the fire-threads, but she wasn't sure what the result might be. The fiery cloth did cast a strong light on her work area, and wasn't that the important thing? She left it alone.

Using her hammer, she resentfully tapped a groove into her iron rod. Where would she be right now, if her family hadn't drowned? Probably south in the Pebbled Sea, underway for their winter berth. The wind, just starting to turn chilly, would be tumbling through her braids, filling her nose with clean salt air—not this dusty, smoky stuff.

Jamming the rod's pointed end into a hole in the metal lump called a nail header, she gave the iron a hard twist. The rod broke neatly where she had cut the groove into it. And our ship wouldn't have a cargo of *these*, she thought, putting the longer piece of rod aside. We'd have, oh, spices from Bihan, and gold from Sotat. Maybe some flower-perfumes from Janaal.

With a hard, quick hammer-blow, she put a flat head on her nail. Lifting the nail header tool at the back of the anvil, she upended it: her finished nail dropped into a water bucket near one of her feet. Steam hissed out in a tiny plume. Sighing, Daja fished for the cool nail and tossed it into a second, empty bucket. With the ease of practice she put the nail header on the anvil, right over the hole made for it. The remainder of the first rod went back into the fire to heat. She grabbed the next iron rod to begin the whole chore over again.

Daja worked steadily, ignoring the sweat that trickled down her cheeks, back, and sides, dreaming of ships under full sail in the Pebbled Sea. She was big for her years, deep-chested and thick-waisted, dressed in a boy's thigh-length black tunic and black leggings. The leather apron that protected her clothes was grimy and spotted with burns. The steady glow of light from her fire-weaving played over skin as brown as mahogany; a wide, full-lipped mouth now tight with unhappiness; and large, deep-set brown eyes. The only touches of color about her were a scarlet armband and red ties at the ends of her braids.

"You are the smith?" a female voice inquired behind her. "I have work to be done."

Daja turned, squinting. At first it was hard to make out the woman who stood in the wide doorway—the sun was at her back, leaving her face in shadow. The only thing clear at first glance was that she had but one leg. The other, cut off at mid-thigh, had been replaced by a sturdy length of fitted wood.

"I'm not the smith," Daja replied.

The whites of the visitor's eyes glittered; she was staring at Daja's fire-square. The girl sighed. People were always so nervous about the ways she and her friends shaped magic! "Sorry," Daja murmured, and flapped a hand at the square. It twisted, becoming a single rope, then snaked back into the forge.

The visitor took two hopping steps into the building. Now Daja saw her clearly, and wished she could not. One side of the newcomer's face was the color of bronze, lit with a single heavy-lidded dark eye. The other side was a ruin of shiny brown scars, the eye only a lumpy pit. Scars dragged at one side of the woman's broad-curved mouth, so that she seemed to be forever sneering. Her nose was unscarred, but something had broken it enough to make it nearly flat. Both of her eyebrows were thick, making Daja wonder if she had been any kind of beauty even before the loss of half of her face. The scarring aside, she didn't look very old—no more than twenty-five at the most.

The newcomer wore an earth-brown tunic that reached halfway down her thighs. Like Daja, she wore leggings. They were the same dark color as her tunic, with one leg shortened to cover the joining of the wooden leg to her flesh. Daja noticed all of this in an eye-blink. The thing that brought her mind to a halt was the brass-capped staff the woman leaned on.

She was a Trader.

Daja's belly clenched. She tried not to stare hungrily at the etchings and metal inlays that decorated the cap on the visitor's staff, the marks that told those who knew how to read them of the woman's family and deeds. Now that she was *trangshi*, Daja wasn't supposed to care about things like that, but she couldn't help herself.

The woman scowled and thumped the ground with her staff as she took a more comfortable position. "What's the matter, *lugsha?*" she demanded in a deep, pleasant voice, using the word—only slightly complimentary—for "craftsman." "Haven't you seen a cripple before? Or just not one so pretty as me?"

Daja lowered her head and waited. As soon as the Trader's eye adjusted to the gloom, this conversation would end.

"No, you're not big enough to be a whole smith. Apprentice, I desire to speak with your master," the woman said flatly. "There is work to be done, and—"

Since Daja wasn't looking, she couldn't watch the Trader examine their surroundings as she tried to spot an adult smith. When the woman fell silent, though, Daja knew what she had seen: her staff, with its unmarked cap.

Daja looked up in time to catch the glare the

11

Trader directed her way. Then the woman turned her face toward the forge.

"Where is the smith?!" she called, her voice ringing from the metal all around them. "I desire to speak with the smith, immediately! There is work to be done, work for which Tenth Caravan Idaram will pay!"

Tris, Daja called with her magic. *Tris, I need you.*

Behind the smithy, Tris sighed. The worst part about helping Daja, as far as she was concerned, was the interruptions. Rather than answer, she reached out and gripped a fistful of air. Giving it a twist, she threw it like a spear through the opening in the wall. That done, she ran nail-bitten fingers through her very short red hair, thrust her brass-rimmed spectacles higher on her long nose, and went back to reading.

Inside the smithy, flames roared like dragonfire out of the bed of hot coals. The Trader flinched.

I don't need more air! Daja informed her friend. *I need help, right now!*

I'm busy, came Tris's reply. *Get someone else.*

There isn't *anyone else.*

"I have no choice but to stand here and hope that someone will tell me where I can find the smith," the Trader announced, turning her back to Daja. If Daja spoke, she knew that the Trader would pretend not to hear: that was how Traders handled *trangshi*. "It is most urgent that I speak to a smith—to a *real* smith."

12

Trisana Chandler, I need you right now! thought Daja fiercely.

Furious, Tris rose, shook out her skirts and petticoats, and closed her book and stuck it into the pocket of her gown. Sparks glimmered at the ends of her hair as she stomped around the side of the building. Coming to a halt beside the Trader, she scowled up at the woman with storm-gray eyes. Her pale, lightly freckled skin was blotched red and white with anger; the two-inch strands of her coppery hair were rising to stand at angles to her head.

"What do *you* want?" she demanded. "I was *reading*."

"I want the smith," the Trader snapped back. "I am Polyam, *wirok* of Tenth Caravan Idaram. I have business for him."

"The smith is out riding with the duke of Emelan," Tris replied. "There's my friend Daja Kisubo. She's all the smith you'll get till they come back!"

"I'm *trangshi*, remember?" Daja asked patiently. "By Trader law I don't exist. If I don't exist, then she can't talk to me or hear me. Get hold of yourself, will you? You're sparking all over the place."

Tris raked her fingers through her hair and examined the fistful of light she had gathered. "Shurri defend us," she muttered. Closing her fingers, she killed the sparks.

Polyam backed away from her. "If I had a choice, I

13

would go somewhere else," she informed Tris. "But I don't. It's two days' journey to the next blacksmith on this road. I will wait until this smith comes."

"Why don't you tell me what you want, and I'll tell Daja," Tris said, a shade too patiently. "Then she can do what you need and you can go away with your whole caravan."

"If a *trangshi* were here, I could not accept work from that *trangshi's* hand," replied Polyam. "Even if you handled it before me. I must have a smith. One that is not unclean."

Now tiny lightning bolts rippled over Tris's hair and around the frames of her spectacles. The Trader clung to her staff with both hands, her dark face ashy with fear.

"She's a *xurdin*, not a *yerui*," Daja said quickly. She knew Polyam heard, but there was still custom to observe—she wouldn't admit that she had. "Tris, tell her you're a *xurdin*, a mage. She thinks you're a *yerui*, a hungry ghost-devil. That your magic will eat her. *Please*," she begged, knowing her friend was about to refuse.

The other girl sighed. The tiny bits of lightning began to shrink. "I'm a mage, all right?" she said to Polyam. "I'm a mage; she's a mage. It's just strange magic we have; it's not like most people's. It's not evil; I won't hurt you. I'm *trying* not to hurt you right now, and I'm succeeding, aren't I?"

Polyam's full mouth tightened. "You didn't have to

14

tell me your magic is strange," she replied. "I've been on the roads all my life, and I've never seen anything like what you just did."

Daja came up to stand at Tris's back. "I'll see if Sandry or Briar can get the smith," she whispered into her friend's ear. "Be polite. It's not *her* fault I'm *trangshi*. Offer her water from the well."

Tris glanced back and up into Daja's eyes. "It's not your fault, either."

"It doesn't matter, not if you're a Trader. Offer her a drink." Daja stepped into the shadows behind the forge. Perhaps if Tris couldn't see Daja, she wouldn't be so quick to defend her against what she saw as insults.

She's only a *kaq*, thought Daja tiredly. It was the first time in weeks that she'd thought of the redhead that way. Tris wasn't so bad, once you got to know her, but *kaqs*—those who weren't Traders—didn't understand important things like *trangshi* custom.

Sandry, Briar, Daja called, sending her magic through the air. *Can you find the smith, Kahlib? He's got an important customer who will only talk to him.*

Nearly two miles away Lady Sandrilene fa Toren inspected a heavily embroidered jacket. It belonged to one of their warrior escorts, who had draped it over a tree-limb while he and his friends watered their horses at a mountain stream. Sandry had wanted a better look at one of those jackets all morning, ever

15

since Lady Inoulia of Gold Ridge and her people had joined the duke on their inspection of the largest grassfires. No doubt the man would have let her see it if she had asked, but that would have involved bowing and respectful conversation with Sandry as Duke Vedris's great-niece. She would have felt guilty about keeping a nervous man standing as she went over the beautiful needlework on his back. It was simpler this way, with the tree to hide her slender form from the warriors at the brook.

She brought her small nose close to the stitches, marveling at the complex embroidery. All the riders' jackets started with the same image: a lavender flower, well opened, with slender yellow rods at the center. Each design, though, was individual in the waves of light that radiated from the design, done in all colors, patterns, and threads. She had stopped doing fine embroidery more than two months ago, but these jackets made her fingers itch to pick up needle and silk again.

She was a slim, fine-boned girl, with bright blue eyes and a stubborn chin. Sunstreaks gilded her brown hair, tidily braided and pinned up under a sheer gray veil. Her overgown was dove gray linen, sleeveless and plain but for a long row of jet buttons down the front. Jet buttons also twinkled atop her small, black shoes. Her puff-sleeved undergown was white cotton, woven so fine as to be almost comfortable in the stuffy heat of the day. She would have loved to trade this elegant mourning for just one of her light cotton dresses, but that would have shocked the nobles who housed her great-uncle and his companions on this long ride through Duke Vedris's realm. Sandry did not feel like explaining that her parents, dead a year, would have laughed at the thought of her wearing deep mourning, as was expected of the nobility. Instead, as long as she rode with the duke, she wore the clothes proper to her station and envied her three friends their freedom to wear colors and fewer layers as she herself did at home.

She thrust her discomfort from her mind and peered more closely at the ornate embroidery. Could *she* do that braided stitch?

"If you want me to nick it"—Sandry jumped, and the boyish voice went on—"I'll have to wait till dark."

She glared into Briar Moss's amused green eyes. "As if you stole *anything* anymore!" she retorted.

"Now *that's* where you're wrong." Reaching into the loosely belted brown jacket he wore instead of a shirt, he produced two small bunches of grapes. "The best around, with the crops falling off." He passed a bunch into her hands. "I've had better."

Sandry returned the grapes. "Thanks, but no. Watch for those riders coming back."

He glanced at the brook. "Don't worry. They've

17

taken off their boots and they're cooling their toesies. Maybe I *could* nick the jacket right now, if you want it."

Sandry shook her head and returned to examining the embroidery. Briar leaned against the tree and ate his grapes. Unlike her, he was dressed for comfort: he wore cotton breeches and normally went barefoot, unless one of their teachers forced him into sandals or boots. At five feet, he was taller than Sandry by a hand's length. He had the glossy black hair—worn short and rough-cut—almond-shaped eyes, and gold-brown skin of an easterner, but a thin-bladed nose and eyes that changed from gray-green to lime green pointed to western blood in one of his parents. He wasn't sure which of them it might be: he had never known his father, and his mother had died when he was four.

"I thought all the grassfires would be hurting you and Rosethorn," Sandry remarked as she traced a metallic thread in the pattern of stitches.

Briar shook his head. "The grass is mostly dead." He'd left Rosethorn, his teacher of plant-magic, calmly discussing next year's crops with the duke and Lady Inoulia. "Their drought killed most of it weeks ago. And the top burns so fast that the fire moves on, and the roots and seeds are fine, still."

"Oh," Sandry murmured, not really listening. "What flower is this? On these jackets?"

"It looks like a crocus. Why?" He wasn't vexed

18

with her for not listening. He knew what she was like when she saw anything unusual done with cloth.

"Just curious. Here, look at this thread. Is it real gold, or—"

Sandry, Briar. Daja's magical voice made them jump with surprise. Heat jumped from Sandry's finger to race down the metal thread, melting it as the silk around it charred. She gaped at the mess. She had no fire or lightning magic—that was Daja and Tris! How did she melt that thread? And what could she say to the jacket's owner?

I'll find the smith, Briar told Daja. The sense of contact with her faded. "C'mon," he urged Sandry.

"I burned it!" she hissed, grabbing his sleeve and pointing out the scorch marks. "I was touching it when Daja reached us and—and *heat* came out of me!"

He scratched an elbow. "All the more reason to leave before the owner sees it."

Sandry shook her head. "It's my fault the jacket is ruined. I have to make amends."

"Why?" he asked reasonably. "Nobody saw you—"

"*I* saw me," she said flatly.

The boy stared at her. "Nobles," he finally remarked. "You don't see *me* having a conscience." He looked at his jailhouse tattoos, black X's stained deep into the webs between his thumbs and forefingers. "It just confuses things."

"They're coming back," she said with a nod toward

the creek. The men had finished their gossip, and the jacket's owner was approaching. "You'd better go find the smith."

"You expect me to leave a mate in a pinch," he replied scornfully. "Don't *you* see me nice!"

"It's not that," protested Sandry. She stood up straight, shoulders back, chin up, and folded her hands neatly in front of her.

The man who had left his jacket there halted with a frown. "Excuse me, my lady," he said, reaching for his property. He said nothing to Briar, but kept an eye on him.

"I ruined your jacket," Sandry told him, her upper lip quivering. "I can't explain it, but you had a metal thread in the embroidery, and it melted. What repayment would be fair?"

"You melted a thread," he repeated, one black eyebrow raised. "I don't see a fire here." He was a handsome young man, with the long black hair and slanted black eyes common to these mountains. The hint of a smile twitched the side of his mouth.

"Magically," replied Sandry. "I'm pretty sure it was magically. The design was so beautiful, and now it's scorched and that thread is gone."

There were muffled chuckles from the warrior's friends. He examined the design. "Looks like a kind of spiral fern, doesn't it?" he asked his companions, showing them the scorched mark. "One just unfurling."

20

Briar had to admit, the design didn't look ruined. A thin, spiky burn mark wound about the crocus and across the bands of color that radiated from it. Someone could have etched the mark in deliberately.

"Doesn't seem damaged at all, my lady," said one of the rider's friends.

Sandry gulped. "I could make a new design, and replace that," she told the jacket's owner. "It would take me a while, but if we're in these mountains for a few weeks . . ."

He shrugged the garment on. "I like it as it is." Picking up her hand, he bowed and kissed her fingers. "I'll be the envy of my village, with your mark on me."

Sandry blushed crimson. The rider winked at Briar and walked away.

A few of the other warriors stayed. One removed his jacket and offered it to the girl. "Would you do mine?"

She shook her head without looking up. "I don't know how I did it—and if I did, I don't know that next time I wouldn't burn the whole thing up."

The riders looked at each other and shrugged. "If you figure it out, I'd like to know," said the one who'd offered his jacket. The men bowed to her and went off to find their horses.

Sandry looked at Briar. "I need to find an answer to this accident," she told him. "Otherwise, what's to say I won't destroy something?"

*　　*　　*

After pointing out the well to Polyam, Tris had returned to her seat and her book, still bristling over the Trader's behavior. She was just beginning to calm down when a shadow fell over her page. Looking up, she saw Polyam. "Now what?"

"*Our* children have better manners," the woman said tartly as she thumped the ground with her staff, trying to find a better place to stand.

"Then go bother one of them," muttered Tris. She went back to her reading.

One end of the staff—the dirty end, she thought indignantly—tapped the pages of her book. "I have a name: Polyam. Use it, and tell me something, *xurdin* girl. If you knew one who was not a Trader—who was *trangshi*—would you also know why?"

Tris brushed dirt-flakes from her book. "What do you care? *Polyam*," she added when the Trader glared at her.

Polyam lifted the end of her staff and held it close to the book. "A polite answer is noted by Oti Bookkeeper, and is entered in the account-book of your life. I have nothing to do until the smith comes but keep my face in front of yours, if you would rather be rude than tell me what I ask."

Tris looked up at the Trader's scars, and looked away.

"I'm not pretty," said Polyam grimly. "A *wirok* doesn't need looks. People are very happy to give me what I want cheap and send me away, rather than

22

have me about. I ask again: If you know one who is *trangshi*, would you also know why?"

Tris gnawed her lip and decided she would rather that this woman with her torn face and missing leg go away. "The ship Daja's family was on—Third Ship Kisubo, it was called—it sank. She was the only survivor. Now she lives at Winding Circle temple. *You* people kicked her out like the wreck was her fault."

"You do not get rid of someone with smallpox because it is that one's fault. You do it so no one else will get the disease. Bad luck is a disease. Only the carrier—a *trangshi*—survives it, to give it to others."

"Nonsense," retorted Tris.

"You are sure of many things, for one who is not very old." Polyam sighed and muttered, to herself more than to Tris, "I may be *wirok*, but at least I am still *Tsaw'ha*."

"What does *wirok* mean, anyway? And saw-hah?" Tris always wanted to learn the meanings of new Trader words. Unlike her friends, she couldn't speak Tradertalk. "And what's so wonderful about being that and not what Daja is?"

"*Wirok* bring no profit to the caravan," was the reply. "A *wirok* spends the caravan's money with blacksmiths, and food sellers, and other needful *kaqs*. Even our children scorn a *wirok*. And you call *Tsaw'ha* Traders."

Tris lifted her pale brows, her gray eyes puzzled. "Being a *wirok* is still better than being *trangshi*?"

23

The Trader hesitated. Whatever reply she might have made was lost when Daja shrieked inside the forge. *Tris!* came Daja's frantic mind-call. In all the months Tris had known her, she had never heard Daja sound as terrified as she did now. *TrisTrisTRIS!*

The redhead jumped to her feet and raced into the building. The moment she saw Daja, she skidded to a halt.

Inside the smithy, Daja could hear Polyam clearly. Eavesdropping, not thinking of what she was up to, Daja had gone to draw a fresh nail-rod out of the fire. Instead of one length of iron, she had grasped the entire fistful of rods she'd set to heat.

Once in her grip, unnoticed by Daja, the rods had twined around each other, then split apart, forming three branches. One branch reached toward the fire, splitting again to form three twigs. Another branch wound itself around Daja's arm.

Startled by the feel of iron on her skin—though she could handle red-hot metal without getting burned, the sensation was an odd one—Daja looked down. A third iron branch reached between the fingers on her free hand, then wrapped around her palm and over her wrist.

Daja tried to pull free and failed. She bent her power on the iron, silently ordering it back to its original shape. Instead the pieces that gripped her arms continued to grow. They each seized a shoulder, holding it fast. One spread down her back;

another sprouted a tendril that gently twined around her neck. That was when she panicked and screamed.

When Tris reached her, she found Daja trapped by what looked like an ancient grapevine—trunk, limbs, and all—made of iron that still glowed orange with heat. It was sprouting metal leaves.

"It's *growing*," Polyam gasped. She had followed Tris back to the forge.

"I can see that!" growled Tris. "Now hush—I have to do some magic." *Frostpine!* she cried silently, calling through her magical connection to her friends. They needed Daja's teacher, and they needed him now. *Briar, Sandry, get Frostpine, hurry!*

"Tris, make it stop," Daja begged. "I can't—magic won't touch it. *My* magic—"

Tris felt Briar's and Sandry's magics flower in her mind, as if they stood within her skull and saw through her eyes. She wished that Frostpine were part of their link. Things would be so much easier if she could speak to him as she did to her friends.

Briar, it's got leaves, it's yours, Sandry announced. *Do something. Tris, open to him. To us.*

"Daja, breathe deep," ordered Tris. "Calm down. It's harder to work if you're—"

"How calm would *you* be?" the captive demanded.

Tris hesitated, then grabbed Daja's hands. Briar and Sandry concentrated. Using their intertwined magics, following the ties that stretched between all four of

25

them, they reached into Daja with Tris, pouring in to fill Daja's skin.

I never made anything not *grow before,* Briar told his friends. *And the metal confuses me.* He spread through the girls, reaching into the limbs of the iron plant. All of them felt him twine around Daja's power, blocking the tendrils as the metal reached for more growth. All of them felt him grip, gathering the spreading power into his fist, and twisting it around. When he released it, the magic was locked in place.

Tris and Daja opened their eyes. The iron vine had stopped growing.

It had also wrapped its tendrils around Tris's hands. Tug as she might, she could not pull herself free of Daja.

2

An hour later, the smith-mage Frostpine inspected Tris and Daja, stroking his wild beard and trying to look serious. A dedicate of the Living Circle temples, he wore the red habit that meant his vows were given to the gods of fire. He was muscular, an inch or two over six feet tall, with skin a deeper brown than Daja's, dark eyes, and full lips that liked to smile. Bald on top of his head, he grew his wiry black hair long on the sides, as if to make up for it. His heavy-lidded eyes glittered now with what looked suspiciously like amusement.

"I suppose nothing like this ever happened to *you*," Tris accused sourly. She and Daja were still trapped.

Before she had left them, Polyam had found a tall stool for Tris to sit on. Daja could not sit—the metal had grown down as far as her thighs, making it impossible for her to bend.

"Actually, my power got away from me once. I was—" Frostpine cleared his throat. "I was attempting to put some gold ornaments back onto a tribal queen's jeweled collar."

"She gave him her gems, and he knew that her husband would miss them and suspect that she had given them to a lover." Rosethorn leaned against the wall, arms crossed over her chest, her delicately carved mouth curled in a half-smile. Sandry and Briar sat on the ground next to her.

"I didn't know she was married," said Frostpine defensively.

"Did you ask?" Rosethorn inquired. She was a stocky woman only an inch taller than Daja, with short-cropped chestnut hair and wicked brown eyes. In her green habit, which marked her dedication to the gods of the earth, she was hard to see in the shadowy forge.

"Not all of us are as perfect as you," said Frostpine, putting his hands on the iron that held Daja and Tris captive. "Sometimes magic gets away from a mage, is the point I was *trying* to make." He glared at Rosethorn, then concentrated on his task.

Daja smiled. Frostpine would make things right.

He always did. She could feel the power that welled from him as his magic fed into the iron vine.

"There." Polyam had come back to the smithy. This time she brought company, two other Traders: an older woman who wore a gold-trimmed maroon gauze veil on her hair, and a *mimander*, a Trader mage, robed head to toe in lemon-colored cloth, wearing a face-veil of the same eye-smarting shade. "It is as I told you," Polyam said to them.

Daja felt her teacher's power draw back as Frostpine glared at the newcomers. "I don't mind if you watch, but you must be silent. We don't need distractions."

The older woman nodded as regally as any queen; the *mimander* bowed. All three Traders, including Polyam, leaned on their staffs as they watched.

After a moment, Daja felt Frostpine's power return to the vine. He was putting forth more effort now. "You know, I expect liveliness from gold," he murmured to her. "It's such an agreeable metal, and it takes suggestions a bit too well. But iron? Iron shouldn't be getting into this kind of mischief—aha!"

No one had to ask why he had exclaimed: the metal vines were shrinking, pulling away from the girls' captive arms. Tris yanked free. The vines loosened their grip on Daja more reluctantly, but eventually they let her go. She slid out of their hold with a

29

sigh of relief. The moment she was loose, she and Frostpine drew their magic from the iron.

"*Now* what do you do with it?" Rosethorn wanted to know. "It seems a shame to melt it down."

The iron tendrils coiled, shrinking away. "I think you scared it," Tris remarked.

Daja picked up the metal plant. "I don't know if we could make anything normal with it even if we did melt it down." She ran her fingers over the corded trunk. "It doesn't exactly feel like iron now."

Rosethorn put a hand on one of the branches. A thin iron twig sprouted between two of her fingers. "*I* think it's going to keep growing. That's how it feels to me."

"You are *certain* that it will grow?" asked the *mimander*, his voice slightly muffled by his yellow veil. He walked farther into the smithy, bowed to Rosethorn and Frostpine, and held a yellow-gloved hand over the iron vine. "Yes—I can feel the power. This is like nothing I have known."

"May we help you, honored *mimander*?" Frostpine inquired.

The older woman spoke quietly to Polyam, who announced, "Tenth Caravan Idaram will pay, in the coin of Emelan, a gold maja for this thing."

Daja frowned at the Traders. A gold maja was half a year's income for a poor family. That was startling enough. What was more startling yet was that she knew Trader custom: that sum had to be the lowest bid the newcomers could think she might accept.

"It must be cleansed of contact with a *trangshi*," the *mimander* remarked to Polyam and the other Trader.

"It was a *trangshi* that made it," snapped Rosethorn. Tris beamed at her.

"Even a rat has fur and meat," Polyam replied, her eyes bright. "A gold maja and a gold astrel. We would offer more, but there is the cost of the herbs and oils for the cleansing to be considered."

Three hundred silver crescents! Sandry told Daja through their magical tie. *It's a dowry, or new tools, or even gold to work with. Maybe you ought to take it?*

Think it over, Briar advised. *You have something they want. Make 'em pay through the nose. That's a fine revenge, after how Traders dealt with you.*

"It's not for sale," Frostpine told Polyam and her companions. "We need to study it before *any* decision is reached."

"A gold maja and two gold astrels," the older woman said. "Not a copper more. The *trangshi* may have the night to consider it." She walked away, head high. The *mimander* hesitated. He might have been looking at Daja, but it was hard for her to tell through the fine yellow veil on his face. Then he, too, followed the older woman. Polyam shifted position to let him go by.

"You needn't think *gilav* Chandrisa will go up from that price," she said to Frostpine. "Hers is the last word in any bargaining."

What's a gilav? Tris inquired silently.

Caravan boss, answered Briar. *Like the captain of a ship.*

Daja looked at her vine. One tendril had wrapped around her finger, catlike. She felt a bubbling emotion in her chest, one that threatened to cut off her breath. They can't have it two ways, she told herself. Either I don't exist, or I do. They must want this very badly, to make an offer to a *trangshi*.

"We Blue Traders have a saying," she remarked, staring off to Polyam's side. "When three parties bargain, no one wins. Tenth Caravan Idaram must bargain with me directly. *Me*. Talk to Daja Kisubo the *trangshi*, or there will be no talk at all."

Frostpine grinned and put an arm around her shoulders. Sandry clapped; Briar whistled his approval. Even Rosethorn and Tris smiled.

Polyam shrugged. "Since I heard nothing, I can transmit no offers that are impossible to meet." Turning, she hobbled off after the other Traders.

Daja tightened her grip on the iron, wishing she could go with them, could return to the kind of life where she had always known the rules.

We're *your people now*, Sandry told her in mindtalk.

They threw you out, added Briar. *Or were you forgetting?*

"Frostpine!" A short man with gray-bristled cheeks stood in the doorway, glaring at them through dark eyes buried in wrinkles. He dressed like a craftsman in a knee-length green tunic, loose brown breeches, and leather slippers; a round white cap covered his hair. "I never bargained for your *apprentice* doing magic here, all unsupervised."

"Neither did we," Frostpine said, walking toward the owner of the forge with Daja in tow. "Daja Kisubo, this is Kahlib ul Hanoh, the village smith."

Daja hoisted the iron vine into a better grip. Bowing, she nearly fell over, unbalanced by her creation. "Sorry about the magic," she said, red with embarrassment.

"I hope you didn't leave any loose—it acts oddly, if it isn't used in the working," chided the smith. "I'm not a mage, but I've dealt with them enough to know."

"I think it's all in the vine," muttered Daja, looking around. They had learned to see magic over the summer, a useful side effect of their magic coming together. She used that vision now, but the only silver gleam of power she could find was on the mages.

Frostpine clapped her on the shoulder. "Why don't you go back up to the castle and have a bath?" he suggested. "You look wrung out."

She was also filthy, Daja realized. Soot from the iron vine streaked her skin and clothes from her neck to her knees. Even for a smith, that was a lot of dirt. "All right," she said quietly.

"Take that with you," ordered Kahlib. "I don't have time to keep an eye on it."

Daja settled the branching iron in her arms, bowed again to the smith, and trudged out of the forge.

Rosethorn turned to Briar. "Now all the excitement's over, student of mine, how would you like to see the gold of Gold Ridge?"

Five months ago Briar had been a street-rat and thief: the mention of riches still had power over him. "*You* want to show me gold?" he asked. "You don't have any use for it."

"This kind I do. Come on." With a polite farewell to Kahlib, Rosethorn drew Briar outside and led the way in the walk up the road to the castle. The dog Little Bear sat in front of the gates, plainly waiting for one of his people to return. When Rosethorn and Briar turned short of the dog's post, following a lesser road that headed up into the rough ground south of the castle, Little Bear followed them.

Their new road narrowed until it was more of a track, broad enough for two people to ride abreast. Steep and twisty, it led deep into huge rock formations.

"What kind of gold would they keep outside the walls?" Briar demanded, toiling along. He hadn't thought anything else would be up here—what kept bandits from attacking the castle from behind?

"You'll see."

Rosethorn said nothing more, and Briar saved his breath for climbing. At least the view through the breaks in the rocks was pretty, or it would have been if so much of the valley below had not been hidden in smoke. When the trail leveled off, Rosethorn stopped for a rest, coughing. Even Little Bear sat, his tongue hanging from the side of his mouth.

"Are you all right?" Briar asked his teacher gruffly. He didn't want to seem mushy or anything, but sometimes at night he woke up cold and sweating from dreams that something had happened to Rosethorn.

She took a water bottle from her belt and drank, then rubbed the mouthpiece on her sleeve and passed the bottle to him. "Blasted smoke," she explained after a few breaths. "And the air's thin this high up. Take a look." She waved an arm to her right, where the ground dipped. Briar walked over and blinked to make sure he wasn't seeing things.

Here on the mountain's edge someone had carved out a pocket valley and terraced it. To the northeast, where the far rim should be, he saw a stone wall, manned by soldiers. So much for anyone sneaking up on the castle from behind, he thought, squinting at the small valley. They would have to come over that wall, which looked difficult.

In the pocket valley, rows and rows of plants stood between irrigation ditches that were almost dry. To Briar's sorrow, the plants were all sere and brown, dead or dying.

"The gold of Gold Ridge," Rosethorn commented, sounding better. "Or what's left of it."

"How can plants be gold?" he asked.

"These are saffron crocuses. The flowers' stigmas are worth more than their weight in gold. It takes twenty thousand of them to make up an ounce of saffron."

Briar whistled soundlessly. Saffron was the most expensive spice in the world and made fortunes for those who dealt in it. The cost of a pound of it would probably feed all of Gold Ridge for a year or two. "Gold is right. What happened—not enough water?" he asked without taking his eyes from the terraces before him.

"What they have they bring up from the castle, but that's hard water and isn't very healthy for the plants. Usually water isn't an issue—saffron doesn't need much—but the drought has gone on in this part of the country for three years."

"I wish they had let us know earlier this summer," said a light, crisp voice nearby. "We might have been able to help."

Briar jumped. A man walked up to them around a curve in the trail that led into the pocket valley. He was ten inches taller than Briar's own height of five feet, slender, with long hair streaked black and gray. At fifty-three he was older than Rosethorn by twenty years, with a craggy face and a bushy salt-and-pepper mustache. His eyes were his most interesting feature: black as sloes, they were framed with thick black lashes and set deep under heavy black brows. He was dressed well, in a pale yellow linen shirt, loose brown linen trousers, polished boots, and an open cotton overrobe dyed an exacting shade of bronze.

Little Bear whipped the path with his tail, raising a cloud of dust that made Rosethorn sneeze.

"Niko, you scared me out of a season's growth!" snapped Briar, angry at himself for not sensing that another person was nearby. "For somebody whose whole life is about seeing things, you go invisible real fast!"

"That was my intent." Niklaren Goldeye's smile was half hidden under his mustache. "I know I've done well if I can surprise *you*, Briar."

The boy sniffed and rubbed his nose on his sleeve. "I was thinking about the plants," he replied. "Poor things."

"Come take a closer look," Rosethorn said, retrieving her water bottle from him. With Little Bear at her side, she led the way into the tiny valley. The man and the boy followed her.

Closer to the terraces and their contents, Briar could see what had grown there: small flowers, not much more than a few inches high. Everything was undersized; he guessed that the leaves and flowers might be somewhat bigger, had they gotten enough water. Stopping by one terrace, he crouched and held an open hand over the ground. It was sandier than the earth in the larger valley below, with good drainage to carry rain away. Gently he ran a dead leaf between two fingers. As if their lives flowed in his own veins, he felt the plants' struggle to bloom only a week ago. It was too dry; the castle water was too hard with minerals. Without soft rain, these autumn-blooming flowers had given up.

"What are you?" he wondered aloud. "Have you anything left to grow from next spring?" Cupping a hand around the base of one plant, he stretched out his magic.

Something popped behind his eyes; heat pressed his fingertips and jumped away. The crocus he touched collapsed in ashes. White heat flooded from him, enveloping all the plants on that terrace. Under the ground, he felt razor-sharp darts of heat as the still-living bulbs fried. The sandy earth itself warmed. Within the length of a slow breath, every crocus on that terrace was burned, and the soil around the crisped bulbs had run together, half melted.

Briar's jaw hung open. Little Bear whined and hid behind Rosethorn.

"That was *lightning*," Niko said conversationally. "Lightning, where it had no business appearing at all."

Slowly Briar pulled out a pocket handkerchief and

used it to pick up a lump in the dirt. The lightning's heat had turned parts of the sandy ground into glass.

"I don't do lightning," he protested, looking at the sun through the warm glass. The light showed him bits of dirt and plant matter inside the glob. "That's Tris."

"Looked like lightning to me," Rosethorn pointed out.

Briar stared at Niko. "You have to do something about this," he told the man who had brought him to Rosethorn. "I can't go around killing plants. I *can't*." Dismayed, he looked at the pocket of earth he had changed. "And how am I ever going to pay for these crocuses?"

Creeping over to him, Little Bear licked one of Briar's hands.

"Sit," Rosethorn said, putting a hand on the boy's shoulder. "You're white as a sheet."

He obeyed, settling on the rim of the short stone wall that contained the terrace. "Why couldn't it have been rain, if I had to give out magic that's not mine?" he demanded, burying his face in the dog's fur. "There isn't a plant mage born that couldn't use a bit of rain!"

Niko sighed. "Every time I think we have a grip on the things you four must learn, you develop something new." He ran his fingers through his shoulder-length hair. "None of the student mages at Lightsbridge ever broke out like this."

"One of the reasons I never wanted to study magic there," Rosethorn pointed out. "It must be dreadfully tame."

When Briar looked up, startled at what sounded like a joke, she smiled at him. "It's not that bad. Those bulbs wouldn't have made it through the winter— they're at the end of their four years of growth." She stared up at the sky, veiled in its smoky haze. "No one's going to starve because these are finished."

Briar spat on the ground. "I wish we were *home*," he snapped. "I wish we were back in Winding Circle, in our own gardens. Why did we come with the duke, anyway?"

"Because the north's in trouble," Niko said. "He made this trip to see who needs help and how much, remember? He'll require all the aid we can give him to keep these people from starvation when the snows come."

"We may yet fail," added Rosethorn. "Winter comes early up here, and it comes hard when it does. We'd better think of something fast."

By the time she finished the climb up the road from the forge to the castle, Daja was more depressed than she had been in a long time. This was the closest she had come to Traders in months, and they had treated her like dirt. "Like—like *trangshi*," she muttered, entering the castle gate. She could have worked all afternoon not caring that she was covered with iron and soot, but the idea of being too disgusting to talk to had sunk into her pores. She doubted a bath would fix that, but it beat trying to peel off her skin, the only other remedy that came to mind. She headed straight for the entrance to the baths that lay off the main courtyard.

Billows of mineral-scented mist wrapped around her as she walked down a few steps into the underground rooms. The mineral odor came from the water. Unlike the Winding Circle bathhouses, where the water was heated by a furnace, these were filled by a natural hot spring warmed by fires deep within the mountains. Here she could steam the dirt off.

Wrapping the base of her vine in her leather apron to keep it from marking the tiles, Daja propped it against the wall, then went to remove her clothes. Except for a lone attendant, the large chamber was empty. The attendant looked at her oddly as she gave Daja soap, towels, and a scrubbing brush. It seemed no one came here so early in the day. Since she didn't feel like talking, she was grateful for that.

The water was *hot*. She lowered herself into it a breath at a time, letting the mineral-rich liquid take her over. At least the metals in it welcomed her. *They* didn't think she was *trangshi*. Even in this form they wanted her to shape them. Welcoming her, they re-arranged themselves around her body until she felt better. The water cradled her as the sea had cradled Third Ship Kisubo. Daja closed her eyes and let her barriers down.

In her mind she found her iron vine-tree, magic shimmering in each strand, branch, and twig. The metal shifted slowly, spreading a touch here and a hint there. Barely moving, breathing softly, Daja examined her creation. She could feel bits of Sandry, Tris, and Briar mixed in with her own power, but only because she knew what to look for. The time when it was easy to tell her magic apart from that of her friends was over. In the weeks since Sandry had spun the four of them into one so they might survive an earthquake, Daja's fire and metal talents had picked up touches of Sandry's thread-power, Tris's nature-magic, and Briar's connection to growing things. The vine was as much Briar as Daja in its ability to grow, but Sandry's magic had made the rods twist around one another to make a strong trunk. What part of it was Tris's Daja couldn't tell yet, but sooner or later she would know.

So Polyam's *gilav* wanted to buy it—*after* it was cleansed. They would even blame her creation because her family had drowned and she had not. Would she sell it? Frostpine would want to keep it until he understood how it had come about. And it wasn't as if she needed money, not while she lived at Winding Circle. But to have Traders, *any* Traders, talk to her as one of them again . . .

Dream on, part of her said. *You are* trangshi *for life—unless, of course, a miracle happens and a Trader family is so indebted to you that they will* pay *to have your name written in the Trader logs once more. And how often has* that *happened? Once? Twice, in a thousand years?*

She heard voices. With a scowl, Daja opened her eyes.

It was Sandry and her teacher, Dedicate Lark, robed for the bath. They were accepting wash-things from the attendant. Sandry glanced at Daja, then murmured to the servant. The woman bowed and left the room.

While Sandry shed her robe and inched into the steaming water, Lark sat on a bench. Lark's skin was bronze-colored, revealing an eastern ancestor in her family. She looked a bit like a cat, with her broad cheekbones, sharp chin, and short, straight nose. Seeing Lark comb out her short, curly black hair with her black eyes half-closed, Daja expected the woman to purr. An earth dedicate like Rosethorn, Lark was a thread-mage, who worked her power into the things she spun and wove. She and Rosethorn managed the cottage at Winding Circle where the four young mages lived.

Had the new arrivals been Tris or Rosethorn, Daja would have gotten angry all over again, because that was what one did when they were around. Instead she tried to smile when Lark slipped into the pool. "I

43

guess it's silly for a *trangshi* to bathe, since unclean-ness is more than skin deep," said Daja. The joke failed miserably as tears rolled down her cheeks and continued to fall. She closed her eyes, which didn't stop the tears. "If only it was all because of something I *did*."

Lark sighed. "I'm sorry about the Traders."

"At least I understand being *trangshi*, even if I hate it," Daja whispered. "I don't want other Traders to catch my luck." She dashed the teardrops from her cheeks.

Lark put a gentle hand on Daja's shoulder and nodded toward the vine. "Is that your creation, the one they bid so high for?"

Daja nodded as Sandry remarked with pride, "She told them they had to negotiate with *her*. She was splendid!"

"I don't feel splendid," replied Daja. "I feel *un-clean*." Picking up her soap, she began to scrub. "Be-sides, an opening bid means nothing. Only a *hamot* takes the first offer—it's the lowest possible. They only bid gold to start because everyone knows magic drives the price up."

"I don't know what *hamot* means," Sandry ad-mitted. "I never saw much bargaining."

Daja rested her head on the rim of the pool. "It's the kind of person Traders *dream* of dealing with. Someone who's too stupid to know the offered price is insulting."

44

"Hm," Sandry murmured, undoing her braids to wash her hair. "How high do you think they'll go?"

Daja tried to think. "If I knew where they meant to sell, it would help," she admitted. "They must have a buyer in mind." She kicked her legs gently. "If they find a way to talk to me even though I'm *trangshi*, that says I should hold out for three gold majas at least."

"You can buy more scrap iron with that kind of money," Lark murmured. She examined the vine through squinted eyes, then reached out to brush it with her fingertips. "I've never even heard of such a creation. Metal that grows—how big will it get?"

Daja shrugged. "Depends on how much metal's in the soil where it's planted, I suppose. Once it's used all the spare iron in the trunk, it'll need fresh metal from somewhere."

"I hope you make other things like that," Sandry told her. "I think it's *beautiful*."

"Beautiful only because I didn't want the iron for something else," Daja pointed out gloomily. "What if I had? What if someone really *needed* the nails I was supposed to craft? I can't even use this iron again, not with all our magics swimming through it. And what if someone wants me to create another one? This isn't the smithcraft I'm supposed to be learning. I wouldn't know where to start—the magic got away from me when I wasn't paying attention."

Sandry bit her lip. "Mine got away from me this

45

morning, too," she admitted, and told them about the scorched embroidery.

Lark settled back in the water, looking at the girls with interest. "Well. So far the results of your magic veering onto some unknown path have been good, or at least, haven't done any serious harm, but things obviously aren't settling down. The magic in all four of you is continuing to change." She nodded decisively. "It's time to see if it can be mapped."

"How will you map something like magic?" Sandry wanted to know. Her blue eyes gleamed at the thought of learning something new.

"Not *me*, Lady Sandrilene," Lark told her with a smile. "*You*. These changes came about as a part of your spinning. That makes you the best one to weave the map."

Night came early in mountain valleys, earlier than on the heights that surrounded them. An hour or so before supper in the castle, the valley floor was in shadow. From the balcony outside the suite of rooms where Lark, Rosethorn, Niko, Frostpine, and their students slept, Daja watched the bands of dull orange wildfires glow brighter and brighter in the dark.

She knew without looking that the person who had just entered their rooms was Frostpine. "I wonder what could be forged in a blaze like that," she called without turning around. "A bridge over these mountains, or a sword as long as the Emel Peninsula."

"I doubt it. Grassfires don't burn that hot." He

came out and sat on the rail where he could see her face.

A bird dropped from the sky to land on the railing between them. It was a starling, a brown, speckled bird with a sharp yellow bill and clever black eyes. Ignoring Frostpine, it chuckled to Daja, fluffing up its chin-feathers.

"I don't know where Tris is," Daja told the bird. "I think she was in the library all afternoon. Go catch bugs for supper, Shriek."

The bird named Shriek chirped harshly.

"I can never tell if he knows what's said to him," Frostpine remarked.

"The problem is that he's most interested in food, and he always wants that *now*." Daja grubbed in a pocket and came up with some brown bread from lunch. Breaking it up into crumbs, she put them down for the starling. He ate briskly.

"I've been thinking about the work you can do while we're here," said Frostpine, watching Shriek. "We don't want you getting out of practice, and I'm afraid helping Kahlib with his extra work is out of the question for now. It seems the Trader caravan wants him to do some touch-ups here and there."

"And I can't do any of their work 'cause I'm *trangshi*," Daja said bitterly. "So what's left?"

"Both Kahlib and the castle's head carpenter are in need of more nails."

"Frostpine!" Daja protested.

"I know, I know—but that's the best I can manage. Besides, the discipline is good for you. Smithing of any kind, magical or not, is plain hard work."

The door opened to admit Briar and Tris. The moment he saw Tris, the starling began to shrill in the bone-rattling squall used by all fledglings of his breed. Flapping inside to perch on Tris's shoulder, he pecked her ear.

"Shriek, stop! You're a grown bird—act like it!" Flinching, she removed the lid of the small covered bowl that she carried. It was partly filled with tiny balls of raw meat and hard-boiled egg yolk. Bouncing to her wrist, the starling began to gulp them down.

Frostpine got to his feet. "I'd best go put on a clean habit if we're supping with Lady Inoulia," he commented, stretching. "She looks like the kind of woman who cares if people come to the table in work clothes." Passing Briar on his way inside, he tweaked the boy's nose.

Briar grinned, swatted the smith's hand away, and walked onto the balcony, one hand in his pocket. "Want to see something dumb I did?" he asked Daja, producing a lump of dirty, irregular glass.

Daja held it up to the last rays of the sun, inspecting it. Some of those black wisps looked like plant matter, dried grass or root. "Where'd you find this?" she asked.

"I made it," was Briar's glum reply. He leaned against the door to the inside, running his fingers through his hair. "I fried about three silver astrels' worth of dead saffron while I was at it."

Daja figured the amount: he'd *burned* enough saffron to buy a poor family's meals for three months? "Why do a stupid thing like that?"

Tris, joining them, asked, "Yes, why?"

"I didn't *do* it a-purpose," he snapped. "I was *trying* to see if the bulbs were still alive, and—lightning jumped out of me."

Tris held out a hand. Daja passed the lump to her. "The soil in crocus beds is mostly sand," Briar explained. "When I added lightning, I got glass." As Tris examined the lump, her magic causing it to shimmer, Briar added, "If I have to cut *my* hair to stop lightning from growing in it like you did, I might as well shave myself as smooth as Frostpine is on top. It's not like I have extra hair."

Tris's frown twisted into a wry smile. Even with her own hair cropped, she had more of it than Briar.

"*Here* you all are." Sandry came out onto the balcony, pulling three bobbins of undyed thread from her string workbag. "I need you each to take one of these and keep it on you for a day or so."

"Why?" Briar wanted to know, when she offered one to him. "It'll get dirty."

"That's all right," she told him, curling his fingers around a bobbin. "It just has to get to know you."

"Why should we let it get to know us?" inquired

Daja. It felt like plain old silk thread under her fingers.

"Lark thinks I can weave a map of our magics and see where they're getting mixed up," explained Sandry. "It's worth a try, isn't it?"

"What about when we sleep?" inquired Daja. "Our nightgowns don't have pockets."

"Then they go under your pillow," was the noble's firm reply.

"Will this help?" asked Tris, her voice unsure. "Does Lark think it will help?"

Sandry nodded.

"What's to lose?" asked Briar with a sigh. One by one, the friends tucked their bobbins into their pockets.

Lady Inoulia fa Juzon, whose domain Gold Ridge was, dined not alone with those whose rank was closest to hers, but with all the castle inhabitants, noble and servant alike. Sandry refused to think well of the lady for keeping to a custom that many nobles considered to be old-fashioned. She suspected that Inoulia—a cousin of hers by marriage—did it not to make people feel that the lady shared their lives, but to remind everyone who was in charge.

At least Lady Inoulia didn't occupy the highest place on the dais alone, as she had since the death of her husband. Tonight she shared it with her father-in-law, Duke Vedris. Sandry had to smile when she saw her great-uncle incline his shaved head gravely to hear a serving-boy's remark. The duke would listen to anyone, at any time. From Inoulia's frown, she didn't appreciate the reminder. She was the kind of woman who stared into the distance while her servants reported to her.

Sandry wondered if the leaders of Tenth Caravan Idaram, seated at the next table down, might have thought Inoulia was the greater noble if they hadn't already known the duke. The lady wore a cloth-of-gold overrobe and a brown silk undergown with gold embroideries, both of which complimented her dark brown skin perfectly. The gold band on her brown, frizzy hair tilted up a little like a tiara and sparkled with emeralds; black pearls hung in three strands around her neck, and rings drew attention to her long, elegant hands. The duke wore a maroon linen tunic, white silk shirt, and black linen breeches. His only signs of wealth were a gold hoop ring in one fleshy earlobe and a heavy gold signet ring on his hand. To Sandry, Duke Vedris wore command on his powerful shoulders like a cloak. He didn't need gems and precious metals to declare his position.

Lady Inoulia finished a remark to the duke and turned her attention to Sandry. "I regret that pressing duties today made it impossible for me to spend time with you, my dear Sandrilene," she commented. "How did you spend your afternoon?"

52

"I was assembling thread for weaving, cousin," she replied. "I need it for my studies."

Inoulia raised a brow. "Women of our order do not weave."

"You agree, do you not," said an elegant, soft voice over Inoulia's shoulder, "that mages must study that which best enables them to master their power? Sandry's magic is expressed through weaving."

Sandry leaned forward, so she could beam at her uncle. Trust him to hear and come to her rescue!

"Then surely Lightsbridge University is a better place for her to live," Inoulia said to Duke Vedris. "Their mages receive a proper education—like our own dear Yarrun Firetamer and his father, Ulmerin Valeward. I believe most noble houses will hire only university mages."

"A custom I deplore, my lady." Niko, on Sandry's other side, leaned in to meet Inoulia's eyes. "University training does not cover all magic, and unusual power requires unusual teaching methods. Lady Sandrilene can perform prodigies unknown to Lightsbridge."

The expression in Inoulia's eyes clearly said she would believe that when she saw it.

With an inner sigh, Sandry looked over the length of table that stretched between the dais and the main doors of the dining hall. Halfway down, just above the salt-cellar, were Lark and Rosethorn in fresh green habits, and Frostpine in red. At the far end sat Briar,

Daja, and Tris, talking among themselves. Didn't she wish she sat with them!

The main course was over; the subtlety—a spun sugar and fruit peacock, made to be admired, not eaten—had just been presented when the main doors opened. A gray-haired white man entered, leaning on a tall staff decorated with bright enamels. He dressed in much the same fashion as Niko, wearing dark gray silk breeches and shirt and a short-sleeved overrobe of a garnet red velvet, its hems and collar embroidered in black silk. Unlike Niko, he wore his gray hair short; his face was shaved clean, and the scent of expensive soap floated in his wake. Seeing all the guests, he stretched his thin lips in a smile that betrayed no real feeling of pleasure. Sandry, eyeing him, thought that he didn't look all that well. His large, moist brown eyes sported bags on bags, and there was a sallow tone in his skin.

"My lady, forgive me," he said as he walked past the salt-cellar. "I was inspecting the cattle ranges when I heard that his grace the duke had come. I could not be laggardly in paying my respects." He bowed deeply to Vedris. "Your grace honors we northerners by taking so personal an interest in our troubles."

Inoulia smiled. "Your grace, may I present our chief mage, Yarrun Firetamer?" The duke nodded a greeting, and the lady continued, "My dear Yarrun, you have a colleague in my honored father-in-law's party,

Master Niklaren Goldeye, who has been in residence at Summersea."

Niko got to his feet. Yarrun bowed, though not as deeply as he had to the duke. "Everyone knows the name of Goldeye," he said, as if he'd bitten on a sour apple. Niko returned the bow, though if the sideways twitch of his mustache were any clue, he was unimpressed by the newcomer.

Some of these university mages are like overbred cats, thought Sandry, watching Yarrun as the lady introduced the most important of her other guests. They dress to kill and don't want to get their paws wet. Even Niko is a little that way sometimes, especially when he's on his dignity.

Since the diners were almost finished, the new arrival stood on the dais, talking quietly with the duke and Lady Inoulia. They were all about to leave the table when a boy stumbled into the great hall, panting as if he'd been running hard and long.

"Master Yarrun, you're back!" he cried. "Thank all the gods!" He staggered up to the dais, still puffing. Everyone stared at him, noting the burns and soot marks on his rough peasant's clothes.

The duke murmured something to one of the servers, who poured a crystal goblet full of water. The boy gulped its contents between gasps.

Yarrun had drawn back a step, as if to put distance between himself and the messenger. "I take it there is a fire," he murmured.

The boy nodded vigorously, draining the goblet. The server took it back and filled it again as the lad said, "It—it was the croft's chimney, the night drawing down cool and them not cleaning it out first." He took the goblet from the server once more and drank. "Their house is burning. We thought we had it under control, but the wind—"

"How bad is it?" demanded Yarrun.

"Treadwell's roof's burning, and one of the barns. It's in the gardens. If it reaches the wall—you know our wall is just logs, sir—"

Yarrun held up a finger to silence the boy, then pondered for a moment—a *long* moment, Sandry thought, impatient—while everyone in the room shifted nervously. The village at the foot of the hill on which the castle stood was surrounded by forest.

Come on, Sandry ordered the mage silently. *This isn't a play on a stage, it's real people—*

Yarrun smiled brightly. "Would you like a demonstration of my skills?" he asked Niko. "I'm sure you will find it amusing."

Tris's magical voice rang as clearly in Sandry's mind as if the redhead were shouting in her ear. *Amusing! He calls a fire amusing! Why not put a torch to his tail and see if he finds that amusing, too!*

Sandry shook her head, though she couldn't help but think that her grouchy friend had a point.

Yarrun led the way outside. Niko rose and followed, beckoning to Sandry. A glance at Frostpine,

Lark, and Rosethorn called the dedicates to him; Briar, Daja, and Tris ran to catch up.

As she passed behind Inoulia's chair, Sandry heard the lady say to the duke, "This is a small matter, of interest only to those in Yarrun's craft. I thought we might sit in one of the private rooms. Some of my ladies are really quite accomplished musicians."

Is Yarrun so good at this that she doesn't think anything will go wrong? wondered Sandry, joining her friends as they followed the adult mages. Or does she just not care about the village?

Yarrun led the way out of the castle and across the main courtyard, walking briskly. A servant girl caught up with him halfway, delivering a leather bag. Yarrun accepted it and walked on, until they reached one of the thick towers that flanked the main gate. Niko caught up to him there and walked beside him, talking quietly, as they entered the tower. A corkscrew flight of stairs led to the upper reaches and through a door that opened onto the wall.

Since the castle walls were thick, the walkway behind the battlements was a broad one, with guardsmen posted at every hundred feet. From here Yarrun's companions could see an orange glow to the north.

Just like the walls at Winding Circle, these were pierced with deep notches. Yarrun and his guests took positions in them, to be granted a complete view of the night-black ground below, the cluster of huts inside their log wall, and the fire. It was as the boy had said. One house was burning to the ground, while the thatched roof of the house beside it was in flames. Behind them a small barn had also caught fire, upper and lower stories alike. Wide gardens lay between the barn and the wall. They were half-burned, the eager flames seeking every scrap left from the harvest. Everyone drew back to see how Yarrun planned to handle matters.

He turned to Niko, the distant flames reflected in his large eyes. "The courtesy of our craft dictates that I first offer you the chance to douse the flames."

Daja frowned. There was a sting in Yarrun's voice that she didn't like.

"I can't," Niko said quietly.

"Indeed? You are so famous that one would have thought dousing a simple village fire would be an easy matter for you. Are you sure—?" Yarrun asked, raising one eyebrow.

"*Quite* sure." Niko's voice was cold.

The fire-mage opened the leather bag and rummaged inside it. "Then, if I may," he said, drawing out a clenched fist. Walking up to the notch in the battlement, he threw a spray of some kind of powder into the air. Slowly it drifted away from the wall.

Shaping signs with his fingers on the air, Yarrun began to speak in a language the four didn't know. His powder sparkled in the air and sped toward the village below. Yarrun's voice rose, until he spoke three final words in a shout that made Lark cover her ears.

The village fires—the houses, the barn, the gardens—went out. There was not so much as a single glowing ember visible to anyone's eyes. Yarrun slumped against the wall. None of those watching him had any urge to speak, but from below they could hear the distant sound of cheers.

At last the fire-mage straightened. He passed a trembling hand over a face now covered with sweat. Daja thought his brown eyes were larger and wetter than ever. The grin he favored them with seemed half-crazy.

"You were helpless, Niklaren Goldeye!" he remarked, his voice as harsh as a crow's. "You, a member of the governing board of the university, and famous all around the Pebbled Sea! But *I* did it. The fire obeyed *me*."

Niko met the other man's eyes calmly. "You are to be congratulated."

Yarrun sighed. "I only serve the lady of Gold Ridge." He rubbed his eyes. "I had best remain for a while to make sure no pockets are burning in someone else's thatch. This kind of thing is easier under the sun, when I can see the smoke."

"I don't understand," said Briar. "You can see fire better at night."

Yarrun's lips twitched in a false smile. "By the time

we see flames, the structure is most likely doomed. Smoke is the earliest sign there is a fire in the offing. But please, don't linger on my account." He rubbed his hands. "The night grows cold."

It was a dismissal and they all knew it. Briar growled under his breath, resenting Yarrun's attitude. Sandry tugged him along as they followed their teachers into the watchtower.

"He didn't ask *you* if you could put it out," Lark murmured to Frostpine as they began to descend the stairs.

"I couldn't, not at this range," Frostpine replied. "We smiths like our fires up close." He glanced back at Daja with a wink; she grinned.

"Niko, what was the matter with him?" Lark asked. "He wasn't very polite."

"I've seen it before," Niko said wearily. "Some get renown whether they feel they deserve it or not. Others who feel they *should* be famed labor in obscurity. It's—Rosethorn?"

Rosethorn had stopped just short of the ground floor exit. "I'll catch up to you later. I need to talk with him." Gathering the skirts of her habit in one hand, she began to climb the stairs again. The four young people stood back to let her by.

"These academic mages," said Lark as she, Niko, and Frostpine walked out of the tower. "How can you stand to work among them?"

"I do it as little as possible," the four heard Niko

reply as the door swung shut. They were still inside the tower. In the stairwell they could hear the echo of Rosethorn's trotting climb and the creak as she opened the walkway door.

Sandry opened the door to the main courtyard and looked out. Niko and the other two adults were halfway across the yard, heads together as they talked. They seemed to have forgotten their students.

"I wonder what Rosethorn has to say to him?" muttered Briar. "She had that look on her face."

"What look?" Daja inquired softly.

"The one that means she's seen you do something really dumb and she means to pin your ears back," Rosethorn's student answered drily.

Sandry looked back at her friends. She was still holding the door open.

Daja shook her head. Carefully Sandry let the door swing shut.

Not a word was said as the four began to climb back up the stairs. All of them were careful to walk on the outsides of their feet, making as little noise as they possibly could. When they reached the top step, Briar slipped into the lead. Gently, not making even the tiniest sound, he opened the walkway door a crack.

Rosethorn's voice drifted through on the breeze. "—said there hasn't been a forest fire since—"

"It's been thirty years," Yarrun interrupted, sounding as clear as if he stood inside the tower. "My father and I labored for that. Grassfires are one thing. At least *they* are over quickly, and they renew the land. The forest fires were impossible—costly to the fa Juzons and all under their care. My father and I banned them."

"Banned them," Rosethorn repeated, her voice flat.

Uh-oh, Briar said through their magic. *I think it's about to get interesting.*

Rosethorn lowered her voice. The wind picked at the immense house banners that hung over the castle gate, making them flap noisily.

Tris, mind-called Sandry, *fix it.*

The redhead tugged a handful of air as it drifted through the crack; Briar shaped it into a tree-limb that kept the door partly open. Daja gripped one silver-glittering branch and drew it out like wire, shoving it behind her so the strand of air would continue to blow past the four of them and down the stairs. The flow strengthened as Tris pulled more of the outer air through the door. Daja crossed her fingers in the hope that Rosethorn—who was often wise to their tricks—wouldn't notice the small breeze that blew steadily across her face and into the tower.

"Do you know why there are fires in woods and fields?" Rosethorn's voice was clear again, although she fought to keep it to a whisper. "Did it occur to you they might provide a service?"

"Fire serves humankind, my dear young woman,"

said Yarrun, his voice cold and clipped. "Beyond that, it is a symptom of chaos, disorder. Destruction."

"Don't patronize me. I am not 'your dear' anything."

I love it when she talks mean, Briar told his companions. Their grins were all as wicked as his own. They knew Rosethorn's prickles very well and respected them. It was always a treat to see some unfortunate draw her wrath.

"Do not take that tone with me. If you have nothing constructive to say—"

"Deduce something for me, university mage—"

"You Living Circle types are all alike. There is no order anywhere; there is only instinct, and currents, and movement without meaning or structure. Yours is simply a way to avoid study and research—"

"You said it yourself: grassfires *renew the land.* Everything grows back even better than before the fire, isn't that so? Did it never once occur to you or your father that woodlands need fire in the same way?"

"I did not spend the day in the saddle to be lectured by a chanting religious!"

"This valley is a deathtrap." Rosethorn's voice was tight with rage. She took a deep breath. "Fires—small, fast ones—scour the ground of mast."

Mast? Daja asked the others silently.

Junk, replied Briar. *Dead wood, saplings, dead leaves, and nuts.*

Rosethorn was still talking. "Normally an inch or two of that trash burns off fast. The bark on mature trees is thick enough that they survive with only a mild scorching. But now? With no fires for thirty years? The mast is at least a foot thick in most places. Normally it would be wet, damp enough to discourage fire, but you've had three years of drought. It's dry as tinder, your saplings are tall enough that fire in their crowns can now leap to the unprotected crowns of the *big* trees, and everyone here believes *you* can stop such a fire."

"I *can*."

"And if you can't?"

"I have yet to fail, Dedicate Rosethorn. I am very good at my work."

"You have been good at crushing spot fires and warding off lightning strokes. Now you are breeding a firestorm. That won't be so easy to halt."

"And I say you underestimate my power at this!"

"Talk to one of my students about fiddling with nature when it gets in motion. She's still alive to talk about it, but it was a near thing."

"A *child*—"

A hard thumb and forefinger gripped one of Tris's ears. Niko had come up on them from behind, and he did not look pleased. "That's enough," he whispered. "I want that door closed, and then I want all four of you to come with me."

Tris released the branch of air. Briar called the

wood of the door to the wood of the frame, until they came together and the latch caught. Without giving up his grip on Tris's ear, Niko led the four out of the tower and back to their rooms. When they came in, Little Bear jumped up barking.

Niko deposited Tris in a chair. "Sit," he told the three remaining young people.

There was a couch next to Tris that could hold all three of them. Settling on it, they meekly folded their hands on their laps. Niko scowled at Little Bear, who fled into one of the bedchambers.

The man paced, hands in his pockets, heavy brows knit in the blackest frown they had ever seen on his face. His mouth was drawn down tight, the lines around it pulled deep.

"The fault is mine," he said at last. "I never had students so young before. It simply did not occur to me that you would not understand the manners or the common sense that goes with magecraft." He stopped to glare at the four.

"I confess, had I not been so interested in the way your powers combine, I would have called you to book before this," he continued. "Certainly I knew there were other occasions when you eavesdropped on conversations not meant for your ears."

Tris stared at her blue cotton-covered lap.

"Magic is not a toy," Niko continued. "It is not a convenience. It is a precious thing. It is not for use in getting around your elders. I don't believe I realized until we began this trip how often you children call on it when it would be every bit as easy to do things physically instead. You are so strong that you have never learned that you cannot, *cannot* throw magic about like water. That a day will come when you will need every dram of magic you possess, and you will have weakened it to eavesdrop, and play, and do chores that are otherwise boring."

He smoothed his hair back from his face. "As of this moment, none of you are to use magic without one of your teachers to watch you. I mean this. If I suspect you dealt in power without supervision, I will see it on you—you know that I can—and it will go the worse for you."

He examined them all again. None of them would meet his eyes. "This wasteful use of magic will stop before any of us is one day older. Now, go to bed. I am really quite disappointed in all of you."

The castle's farrier was glad to lend his portable forge to Daja the next day. The girl wouldn't have minded working on horseshoes for him, but the farrier had an apprentice, and his smithy was a small one, with no room to spare. Instead Frostpine placed Daja in a little-used courtyard between the castle keep and the outermost wall. As Briar, Tris, and Sandry carried in baskets of charcoal taken from the farrier's supplies, Frostpine gave Daja a fresh bundle of iron rods and left her to the work of making nails.

Yesterday's bundle of iron rods she set against the wall, next to her staff. The iron vine had put out a number of leaves overnight, while the rods that formed its trunk grew thinner and thinner. Little Bear curled up next to it and settled his long frame for a nap. Tris's starling, Shriek, after eating part of a wheat roll and a few insects for breakfast, perched on one of the vine's branches and chattered to local starlings as they flew by.

As he placed his basket of charcoal near the others, Briar sighed with relief. Looking the vine over, he said, "I think you have to plant it in metal-bearing earth, if it's to grow. It has to get new metal from somewhere."

"All I want is to keep it in good condition until I get every copper crescent out of Tenth Caravan Idaram that I can," Daja replied. Drawing a heated rod from her fire, she slid it into the nail header. "After that it can wilt, for all of me." Twisting fiercely, she broke off the rod.

"That's not nice, is it?" Briar asked the vine, running his hands over the trunk. "She doesn't appreciate what a beauty you are, is all. She's used to iron being dead."

"Iron isn't dead!" protested Daja. A stroke of the hammer put a head on the nail; another tap sent the finished piece into her water bucket. "It's just not the same as plants!"

They all turned at the sound of clumsy steps. It was the Trader Polyam coming through the arch that opened onto the main courtyard. Everyone's jaw dropped. The part in her hair, down the center of her scalp, was traced in bright yellow paint of some kind: it ended in a dripping mark on her forehead. Her one good eye was lined in the same color; so too were her mouth, nostrils, and both ears, scarred and unscarred alike. Her neck, wrists, and ankles all sported chains decorated with small wooden charms. Each charm was painted with an odd design in bright yellow. Yellow thread was wrapped around the top of her staff; more yellow thread bound one legging to her wooden limb. Even her toenails and fingernails had been tinted yellow. The color almost seemed to glow, even on the bumps and dents of her scarred face and in the shadow of her ruined eye.

"What happened to *you?*" asked Briar.

"Trader Koma protect me," whispered Daja, forgetting that she had just wrapped her fingers around a rod that was still heating in the fire. "You're *qunsuanen.*" She had heard of the *qunsua* ceremony, its use and intent. Never before had she seen it done—though she knew it when she laid eyes on the results.

"What do you call that shade of yellow?" Sandry inquired. "It's so *vivid.*"

Polyam stared at her for a moment, as if she didn't believe what the girl had asked, then made a face. "I call it yellow." She looked straight at Daja. "Are you happy?" she demanded. "I can now talk to you. I can

69

deal with you. I can even bargain with you. And I will never, ever, acquire enough *zokin* to erase this from the books of the caravan."

"I don't get it," said Briar. "What's koo-soo—what's *zokin*? And the other thing?"

Polyam looked away. Obviously she wasn't about to explain.

"I never heard of the koon-soo thing," remarked Sandry, "but *zokin* is the credit listed against your name in the ledgers of your people. Pirisi—my old nurse—was a Trader," she explained to Polyam. "Pirisi said there are two kinds of *zokin*, the kind that's your actual savings in coin, your part of the ship's—"

"Or caravan's," Daja added.

Sandry grinned at her. "Or caravan's profits. The other kind of *zokin* is, well, honor, or personal standing. Is that the kind you mean?"

Polyam stared at her. "It's not right, a *kaq* knowing so much of our ways."

"She's not a *kaq*," Daja said flatly, staring at the woman. "She is my *saati*." The word meant a non-Trader friend who was as dear as family. "So are Briar and Tris—and our teachers."

"As for *qunsuanen*—koon-soo-ah-nen," Daja repeated slowly, for her friends, "it's, I don't know, she's been cleansed." She felt a little sorry for Polyam. The Traders might as well have named her a plague carrier, to say she was specially privileged to deal with *trangshi*. "All the paint, all the runes on the charms,

70

are to keep my *trangshi* luck from sticking to her. When they go, she has to follow the caravan for ten days, wash in every stream and pond and river they find. The *mimanders* will pray over her and do ritual purifications—"

"As they did all last night," snapped Polyam. She hopped over to the iron vine to take a better look at it. "So let's deal and get it over with. A gold maja and two gold astrels, take it or leave it, *trangshi*."

The word was like a slap in the face. You'd think being *qunsuanen* would sweeten her, thought Daja, breathless with anger. No such luck!

Flame roared out of the forge, shaping a column nearly ten feet high.

"*Tris!*" yelled Briar, Sandry, and Daja. Shriek, grooming his feathers, let out several ear-smarting whistles.

Tris closed her eyes and took a deep breath. The fire sank to its earlier level. Daja went to it to see how her iron rods had fared in the extra heat. They were useless—if she made these into nails, once they were cold they would break at the first blow of a hammer.

"You know, we may be *kaqs*, but at least our manners are good," snapped Tris, glaring at Polyam. "Yours could stand a polishing."

"I'm a *wirok*," Polyam replied, returning the glare with her one good eye. "All I do is spend money among *lugsha*—that's artisans—"

"I know what that one means," retorted Tris.

"And *kaqs*," finished Polyam. "I don't need manners, only authority."

Daja stared at Polyam, thinking she had been stupid to believe it would matter, to speak face-to-face with a Trader again. It was stupid to think her banishment from the world she had lived in most of her life would pinch less if she could pretend she was a Trader just for an hour or two.

She was about to tell Polyam to take the iron vine and keep her money when Sandry rose, smiling her loftiest young-noble smile, and shook out her skirts. She said, "Along with the manners you should use to another Trader—"

"*Trangshi*," Polyam hissed.

Sandry ignored the interruption. "—you appear to have forgotten custom," she continued. "I see none of those things that make it possible to bargain for such a priceless item. Where is the food, and the tea? I'm sure Daja will understand if there are no musicians, given our surroundings. If we were in Summersea, of course, you'd need at least a flutist and a gittern player."

"Cushions," Briar put in, interested. "You need proper cushions to sit on. And one of those little wood table things."

Even Tris was smiling now. "A gift of some kind, as a mark of respect," she added. "Back home in Capchen, the bigger the sale, the more important the token."

Polyam looked at Daja. The black girl was just as surprised as the Trader, but she quickly hid it with a casual shrug. At that moment, Daja thought, she would cheerfully die for any of her three friends, who defended her without being asked.

"Sorry you got all done up in yellow for nothing," commented Briar as Daja put more iron rods into the fire to heat.

"Come back when you are ready to do business," Sandry told Polyam, looking down her small nose at the woman.

Someday I'll have to get her to teach me that trick, Daja thought, watching the uncertainty in Polyam's face. You wouldn't think it possible, but she can go all noble in the wink of an eye.

Without a word, Polyam swung around and left the small courtyard.

Sandry frowned at Daja. "Don't let them walk over you," she ordered sternly. "You're not one of them, so make your own status. If they push you around now, they'll keep doing it, and making you feel bad."

"*And* they'll try to cheat you when they buy," added Tris, who was a merchant's daughter to the bone.

"If you don't let *us* push you around, you oughtn't let *them*," Briar added, practicing a handstand. "We saw you for your own self before *they* ever did."

Daja sighed. "I don't know who confuses me more," she told her friends at last. "You or them."

"Nonsense," retorted Tris, pumping the bellows gently, since she wasn't supposed to use magic to bring air to the fire. "*We* make sense."

"That's what confuses me," said Daja.

"Here," Rosethorn said to a servant behind her. She entered the courtyard carrying a basket full of pointed, spiny-edged leaves. Behind her trooped castle servants burdened with various jars, bowls, knives, ladles, bundles, pots, and a portable stove. A pair of footmen brought up the rear with a long worktable.

Briar screwed up his face. "Awww, Rosethorn," he whined.

The table was placed on a section of the courtyard paved with flagstones, and the other supplies dumped on it. A number of matching blue jars were taken from baskets and lined up: eight of them, all alike, sealed with wax and cord.

"Don't 'awww' me," Rosethorn said, placing the basket of leaves beside the table. "After yesterday I don't want you near the crocuses, but you can still make yourself useful. Those jars—" she pointed to the blue containers "—contain the same aloe-and-oil mixture we make at home. I need you to start turning the liquid into burn salve. You have wax—" She patted a heap of paper-wrapped bricks. "Cheesecloth for straining the liquid, and pots for heating it to blend with the wax. Someone will come with containers for the finished salve in a moment." She settled a lumpy

74

bag with a long strap over her shoulder. "You know the proportions of wax to oil, or you ought to—"

"I know 'em," Briar retorted, and sighed. "After we got rid of the pirates this summer, we did so much of this burn glop I dreamed about it." His hands, giving the lie to his gloomy face, dull voice, and slumped shoulders, cracked the seals on the blue containers.

"Then amuse yourself with salve. Before you start, though, show Tris how to cut up aloe leaves. You'll set a fresh batch to steep in oil while you're at it."

"Urda's womb!" cried the boy. "How much do you want? Enough to *drown* in?"

Rosethorn's eyes were sharp as they met his. "You heard what was said last night, I'm told." Briar grinned sheepishly. "Then you *know* what I expect," she continued, her mouth quivering with amusement. "Look at it this way—maybe if you go to all the trouble of making salve, there won't be a fire. Now get to work." With a salute, she left them. On her way through the arch, she passed a servant with a wheelbarrow full of jars.

"What if I don't want to cut up aloe leaves?" Tris demanded softly.

Rosethorn's voice came back through the arch. "Ask me if I *care* what you want."

"Why?" grumbled Tris. She gave the bellows a gentle pump to keep Daja's fire going at its present heat. "It's not like I don't know the answer." Picking up a knife, she asked Briar, "How am I to do this?"

She had just started to cut pieces of emerald-green flesh from the heart of each leaf when Lark arrived. She carried a basket of her own under one arm and smooth wooden sticks in her free hand. Sandry hurried to take the basket.

"If you want to practice your magic, go ahead," Lark told the other three young people. "We'll be working here all day." Everyone settled into their tasks with very little conversation.

The first interruption came from an outsider. "Dedicate Lark, surely this is not proper work for Lady Sandrilene." Yarrun Firetamer stood in the archway, a thin, unfriendly smile on his lips. His damp-looking eyes were fixed on Sandry, who walked on her knees between three stakes she and Lark had driven into bare earth. As she passed from stake to stake, she unrolled a sturdy thread from a ball of silk yarn. First she wrapped it in a figure eight between the two stakes that were closest together. She then stretched it cleanly around the farthest stake. Back and forth she waddled with her skirts kilted up, grinding dirt into her knees. Her shoes and stockings lay discarded under Briar's worktable.

"You'd be surprised at the work I do, Master Fire-tamer," Sandry told him grimly.

"My dear, you are a fa Toren." He stretched his lips even wider, baring discolored teeth. "You should be at fine needlework, not—*weaving*."

Lark, who was sewing ties to both ends of a wide

76

cloth band, looked at Yarrun. "You say it like it's a dirty word, Master Firetamer. But if I'm not mistaken, that fine robe you wear is the product of weaving—as is every stitch you have on, but for your boots."

Yarrun stroked his overrobe—blue, shimmering silk with multicolored embroideries at the hems—and stopped, as if Lark had tricked him into giving something away. His eyes slid away from her to settle on Briar and Tris. For a long moment he stared, his sallow cheeks turning a mottled red. Briar was straining chunks of aloe from oil. All of his attention was locked onto his task as he carefully poured one jar's contents onto a piece of cheesecloth stretched over a pot.

Tris noticed Yarrun's stare and glared at him.

"Something for you?" she demanded.

"That will make enough burn ointment for an army!" he snapped.

Briar put his jar down and wrapped the cheesecloth around lumps of aloe, squeezing out every bit of oil. Only when he'd finished did he look at the older man. "Dedicate Rosethorn thinks it might be needed." His gray-green eyes sparkled with mischief. "Me, I've learned she's nearly always right."

"I am sure your experience is vast, boy—certainly I, with thirty years as a mage, and ten years' study before that, cannot hope to equal it." Yarrun's voice shook with fury. "You—and your teacher!—are wasting your time!" He stalked out of the courtyard.

"People around here think well of themselves," murmured Daja, striking off a nail.

"We'll fix that," remarked Briar.

"Rosethorn *is* perfectly capable of taking care of herself," Lark reminded them. "Sandry, wait. You're winding too tightly." Going over to the girl, she explained how pulling too hard made the stakes on which Sandry wound her thread lean inward. Sandry nodded, then picked up a mallet and pounded the stakes into a straight line again. If Lark hadn't caught her mistake, she would have finished with a weaving that was shorter on the top than at the bottom.

Daja went to the bellows and gave it a quick pump, watching as strands of fire streamed into the air. They twisted to form a straight trunk, then spread in branches to either side, just as the iron vine had the day before.

They called to her. Reaching almost to the bed of coals, she gripped a pinch of the blue heart-flame in her right thumb and forefinger. Steadily she pulled it up as if she drew thin wire. Starting about an inch above the branching section of fire, she began to weave the blue flame in and out between the orange stems. It was the kind of pattern that Sandry had woven hundreds of times over the summer, the kind of work Daja once used to make a wire net. Reaching the leftmost branch, she doubled back and wove in the other direction. Inside she felt steady and clear, as smooth as a glassy sea with no hint of a breeze to ruffle it. The fire made sense, handled this way. The blue mixed with the orange where they met, providing a small blue spot at every joining, like the heart of a candleflame.

To and fro Daja walked, drawing her blue fire-thread with her, passing it gently through the orange strands. At last she could go no further. She had reached the ends of the orange stems. While she might have pulled them even higher and woven more, she felt a little odd—light-headed, with hot, dry eyes. With her left index finger and thumb she pinched each loose end of fire into the horizontal blue thread until they formed a seamless blend. Unlike her fire grid of the day before, this was far more tightly woven, with gaps less than the width of her little finger between the fiery lengths. The square's brightness dazzled her eyes. Feeling along its base, she encountered the main stem and pinched it off. The fire weaving came free in her hands.

The moment it was flat on her palms, she knew she'd have to put it down. It was much too hot, not to mention too bright. With a sigh of regret, she laid it on the fire.

The fire went out. The weaving blazed against coals gone dead.

"What did you do?" whispered Briar, awed. He, Lark, and the two other girls were peering around Daja.

She glared at him. "Why are you forever asking hard questions?"

He smiled. "Sooner or later you'll have to be able to answer *one*."

Daja shoved him, grinning.

Tris bent perilously close to the woven fire, her long nose just inches from it, her gray eyes squinted nearly shut. "Why did the fire go out?" she asked plaintively. Her eyes watered. "You put this thing on the fire, and it went out, but why? Magic in it?"

"Fire needs air to burn," Niko said, walking over to the forge.

Yarrun was with him. Everyone made way for the two men, who inspected the bright square. "My guess is that your weaving—it is a weaving?" Niko looked at Daja, who nodded. "Your weaving appears to have blocked the air from reaching the coals." He reached out to touch it, but got no closer than a foot. Wincing, he pulled his hand back. "How did this come about?"

"I don't know," whispered Daja, holding her fingers out over the square. Its heat pressed on her skin. "It's just that lately it seems like the fire wants me to do things with it. It *wants* me to shape it. So I do what it wants."

"And yet it's not really fire in and of itself," Niko pointed out. "It appears to burn, yet does so without needing fuel. I suspect it doesn't even need air, unlike your fire." He squinted at the weaving, and the four knew that he was examining Daja's creation with his own power. "It appears to feed on magic, but without destroying it."

Yarrun, who had been pale, was turning a mottled beet color. "This—this is the Great Square of King Zuhayar the Magnificent. The Great Square, but—it cannot be done in fire or in pure magic. Inks, metals, etched in glass . . . I have seen all of these, but . . ." He seemed to be fighting to breathe. "Where are your protective circles? Or runes? What magic can you work if there are no runes to confine the effects or to guide the power of the raising? Niklaren Goldeye, is this your teaching? Magic without direction, without the correct procedures—how can it even exist?"

Lark firmly steered Yarrun to a bench and sat him down. "Get hold of yourself," she ordered, black eyes flashing. "And stop yelling. You don't look at all well. When was the last time you saw a healer of any kind?"

"I don't need a healer!" he cried. "I need explanations! This—this isn't magic!" He pointed at the forge with a trembling hand. "I don't know what it is, but even you Living Circle mages understand there is a proper way to do things, and a Great Square made in fire is not it!"

"Is he always this excitable?" Briar asked Niko, who continued to study Daja's creation.

"He acts like magic's all about rules," added Daja, shooting a glare at Yarrun. Lark had wet down her pocket handkerchief and was putting it across the

81

man's forehead. Yarrun leaned against the wall behind him and closed his eyes. His chest continued to heave; they could see he was talking fast, but at least he had lowered his voice.

"That is the thing about magic," said Niko, smoothing his thick mustache. "It means something different to everyone. The fire *wants* you to shape it, you say?"

Daja nodded.

"What's this Great Square he's talking about?" Tris wanted to know.

"It is a talisman," said Niko. "One generally used to draw things like fortune, wisdom, and the like."

"Goldeye! Are you teaching them by guess and the gods?" Yarrun demanded shrilly.

Niko turned. "Their magic follows no instructional guidelines, or any of the patterns described in *The Encyclopedia of Wisdom*," he said tartly. "My instinct is that to ground them now in matters of runes, protective rites, and formulas would be to restrict the growth of their power."

"Of course it will restrict them!" cried Yarrun, lunging to his feet. Lark's handkerchief fell into the dirt. "Without order to their learning, how will they be tested? How evaluated, how licensed? How will they teach? Even the mages of the Living Circle meet proper requirements to be granted journeyman status, and then an initiate's robe!"

Lark thrust Yarrun back down on the bench and

put her own body squarely between him and his view of the young people and Niko. *"Enough,"* she told him firmly. Lowering her voice, she continued to talk to him.

"Don't let him upset you," Niko told the four softly. "He's old and he's frightened."

"You're as old as him, and *you* aren't scared of us," Briar pointed out.

Niko glared at him. "Thank you oh so much," he retorted waspishly.

"It's not like I mean anything by it," protested Briar. "Nothing bad, anyway."

Lurching to his feet, Yarrun pushed Lark out of his way and stomped over to Niko. "I'm beginning to think those tales I heard of the last few months at Summersea are true!"" he cried. "If these four young people are running wild, I'm not in the least surprised to hear they caused an earthquake!"

"That's not true!" cried Sandry, clenching her hands into fists.

Yarrun scowled at her. "I doubt that you caused a *true* earthquake—not four *children,*" he said with awful emphasis. "Credulous people have plainly blown the entire story out of proportion as it traveled north. But certainly you appear to be running amok—"

Niko swept past Yarrun, one lean arm snaking around the other man's shoulders. "I had no idea that the tales that reached Gold Ridge were so dramatic," he said, talking calmly as he forced Yarrun to keep up with him. "Let's find someplace quiet, and I'll give you the facts of the matter."

Lark was cross for one of the few times that her charges could remember. "Ignore him," she told them firmly, once Niko had led him away. "He thinks the whole world should be ordered as he expects it. Thank heavens Niko got away from the university before they made him into someone like that."

Everyone got back to work without much talk— Yarrun had unsettled them all. Finding that her grid worked as well as a fire to heat her rods, Daja continued to use it: for one thing, it didn't add more smoke to the haze-filled air. Briar finished straining aloe from oil and began to heat the oil and wax to blend them. Tris worked through the basket of aloe leaves, cutting out the moist centers. Sandry finished winding her thread onto the stakes. She and Lark had just transferred the threads to the various long sticks that would serve her as a portable loom when the castle servants brought their midday meal.

5

The midday they got was very different from the sumptuous meal of the night before: hard cheese, cold sausages, bread, and buttermilk. "There's no good complaining to me," the manservant who brought it announced, though no one had said a word. "It's the same fare we all have, though her ladyship would dine better, if she joined my lady and the other gentry in the lesser dining hall."

Sandry shook her head and smiled. "I'll eat with my friends, thank you. Tell her ladyship you couldn't find me, if she asks."

A hint of a smile twitched the man's lips. He bowed to Sandry and left them all to their meal.

"I *hate* buttermilk," complained Tris once they were alone. "And the water here tastes *awful*."

"The bread is stale," added Daja.

"Drought fare," Lark said. "They need to save all they can for the winter. Things will be worse come spring, if they don't get help from outside."

"So fix the drought," Briar said, nudging Tris. "If you can't, who can?"

She made a face at him. "For something that big—something to cover this whole valley? I have to have something to work with, Master Know-It-All. I need wet in the ground, and there isn't any." The girl shivered. "I feel all thin and scraped, it's so dry."

"We passed a lake on our way here," Daja pointed out.

"Did you see how low it was? The lake hasn't enough water to make a difference, and I'd kill whatever's still alive in there. No, thank you!" said Tris forcefully.

"Uncle will help, won't he?" Sandry wanted to know. "He can send grain north, and meat—"

"He'll do what he can," said Lark. "That *is* why he made this trip. The problem is that Gold Ridge isn't the only valley in trouble. The duke's treasury has limits. His purse must stretch to cover all of north Emelan. And the meat and grain merchants can't afford to make loans—they need coin themselves, if they're to buy trade goods come spring."

"Can these northerners even repay a loan?" asked Tris, who took an interest in such things.

"That's going to be a problem," Lark admitted. "Last year, before the drought got so bad, they pledged the saffron crop and the output of the copper mines. This year the crop has failed."

"The mines are failing too," Daja said gloomily. "I heard some of the men talking about it."

"This is too depressing," Briar said firmly as he finished his meal. "At least we'll be well out of it, back at Winding Circle. I heard the duke tell Lady Inoulia he wants to be home before the snows fall."

"There has to be *something* we can do." Sandry looked at the plate on her lap. She'd barely nibbled its contents. Briar leaned over and helped himself to her sausage.

"We're mages," Lark said gently. "We do what we can, but some problems are too big to fix."

"Then I wish I weren't a mage," Sandry replied, her voice low and stubborn. "What good is magic, if you can't use it to help people?"

There was little any of them could say to that. Briar and Tris exchanged looks. They weren't sure they *wanted* to help people for nothing, but there was no way they would admit as much to Sandry.

Not long after he'd returned to work, Briar felt the mildest of cramps. He was shocked, then amused at his shock. How long had it been since he'd eaten food that hadn't agreed with him? Four months? It seemed like four years since his trial and sentencing in Sotat and his trip north to Winding Circle with a stranger called Niko. Only two nights before his trial he'd spent part of the night groaning over a slit-trench, because the chunk of goat meat he'd stolen and devoured had been about a week too old.

There was no sense in complaining—was he a bleater, to whine because the grease in the sausages was off? Instead he excused himself to Lark and the girls and went in search of a privy. A laundrymaid pointed him in the right direction, to another small courtyard where a latrine was set into the outer wall.

Coming out of it, he found Daja kneeling on the ground in the middle of the courtyard. "What're you doing?" he asked.

"Well, I *was* going to use that privy," she replied absently. "I think the grease they cooked the sausages in had turned."

"I noticed," he said wryly.

"But I felt this warm spot. . . ."

He looked at her. She was wearing shoes; he was barefoot. "I didn't feel any warm spots." He walked over to her and put a foot on the patch of ground beside her hands. "It doesn't feel hot, honest."

She shook her head, making her braids dance. "It's there, just a little way down—"

Silver light blazed around her palms. She and Briar flinched.

"What happened?" demanded the boy. Now the ground turned warm under his toes. "What did you do?"

"I didn't *do* anything," Daja protested, sweating. "It just leaped out of me!" Still on her knees, she backed away. The earth was quivering. Something hot was coming up.

The ground where she had been cracked. Steam shot out in a hot, sulfur-smelling cloud, followed by a jet of *very* hot water. Both of them yelped when droplets hit their skins. Warm mist rolled through the courtyard, as heavy as any fog.

A small, dirty hand wrapped around Daja's wrist. C'mon, Briar ordered. *Let's go, before we're seen here!*

Since she couldn't think of anything else to do, she obeyed. Once out of the pocket of steam, they saw they were both covered with mud splatters.

"Cleanup?" she suggested. "Otherwise we look guilty."

Briar nodded, and they dashed for the baths. In the outermost chamber at the foot of the stairs, troughs filled with heated water from the springs awaited those who just needed a quick wash. Both of them scrubbed their arms, legs, and faces, then did their best to remove the stains from their clothes.

"Where'd it come from?" asked Briar, drying his

face and hands on a rough towel. "If you pulled that squirter out of the pipes down here and they're broke, we're in deep dung. And not just with Niko, either."

"I don't know where it came from," she hissed, keeping an eye on the slumbering attendant across the room. "I haven't anything to do with water!"

"No more than Sandry does vines, or I do lightning. Come on, feel around. Maybe we can fix the plumbing if you cracked it!"

Daja glared at him, still rubbing her arms dry, then glanced at the attendant. The woman was snoring.

"You need kettledrums to wake *her*," said Briar.

As if in agreement, the woman snorted and turned away from them on her stool. Now comfortably wedged into her corner, she looked as if she might not stir until the supper bell was rung.

Daja took a deep breath, counting to seven, as she was trained. Briar joined in, closing his eyes as he took up the rhythm. There was her magic, and his, the edges blended together in spots. She let awareness spread, testing for heat where it shouldn't be, or for breaks in the smooth tiles that covered the floor and walls. Metal rang in all her senses: the fixtures in the baths and the pipes. Riding on magic, she and Briar threaded their way through the ground until they found the broad pool of mineral-laden water from which the baths were supplied. They drifted around the immense underground rock chamber the water had shaped for itself.

There Briar split away to let his magic run over the walls. Daja found herself drawn to one of the many springs that fed the pool and dropped through that. She thrust along its length, exploring the walls, discovering a multitude of tiny outlets that bled into the mountains that cupped Gold Ridge Valley.

Sudden heat—much hotter than that of forge or springs, hotter than anything she'd felt in her life—wrapped around her and squeezed. She tried to shout, or thought she did, writhing against that breathless hold. Three months ago she had needed Tris's help to reach the liquid rock that ran far below Winding Circle. Even then they weren't able to touch the lava itself: Tris had called its heat up to where Daja could use it. Now the earth's lifeblood of molten rock and metal had her and didn't want to let her go.

She fought. Heat poured over her, making her edges go cherry red, then start to melt.

A square of blazing white light popped into existence and wrapped itself around her, forcing the lava back. The fire-weaving she had made just hours before was saving her life—or at least, her magical self. Niko was right, Daja thought crazily, it doesn't seem to need any air to burn!

Spying a crack in the rock overhead, Daja shot out of her protective blanket, arrowing straight for the exit. The moment she was free of it, the weaving collapsed, swamped by measureless heat.

Daja zipped through a crack in the earth and into a pocket of water. She was too frightened to stop and get her bearings, or to call for Briar. Escape was the only thing on her mind. Surely there ought to be a way out in this web of seams and cracks, some vent that would take her into open air.

She found it. Coolness washed over her, the gentleness of deep shade: she soared free of the ground. Below her another hot spring bubbled, pool after pool of mineral-rich water and cooking mud. It was cupped in masses of granite. The trees were all pines, which meant she was high up indeed.

For long moments she drifted, letting the cool air ooze through her magical self. *Am I the luckiest girl in Emelan or not?* she thought. *I'd've cooked for certain, if not for a thing I made by accident—by accident!—this morning.*

If it was by accident, she thought again. *I did something almost like it yesterday, just to have some light.*

I wonder if squares like those could be, well, magical shields. I'd have to try them out, though—tinker with them, like Frostpine does with gadgets. What uses might they have?

She gave up such thinking after a while. This was something best talked over with her teacher.

Daja rose higher in the air until she could see an

entire complex of pools and mudpots. Where was all this, anyway? Curious, she flowed over the granite rim of the area around the springs and up a smaller hill, where a herd of shaggy white animals grazed. She stopped to look at them, baffled. Never before had she seen such creatures, though they looked much like *very* large, very shaggy white goats. Thin black horns punctuated the top of their long faces.

You look like a collection of grandfathers, she thought, amused.

Reaching the hilltop, she found she was at the edge of a cliff. Below was a rocky valley. A small river cut it in two along its length.

Cold air drifted by. She looked for the source, and quivered with astonishment. Near her end of the valley lay an immense, jagged ribbon of ice. The valley seemed to continue on under it; the mountains that hemmed the valley also limited that frozen river. It stretched back into those mountains as far as she could see. She tried to guess how deep the center of the ribbon went before it reached the valley floor. It must have been hundreds of feet thick.

Now she heard sounds under the whistle of the wind, an abundance of creaks, groans, and snaps. They rose from the deep cracks in the ice-river's surface, as if the ice either moved or had thousands of residents inside, hammering away. Its depths glinted cool blue. Its surface was filthy, covered with scattered rock and dirt.

What could it be? she wondered. And why did it make so much noise?

Daj'? sounded in her mind. Briar's magical voice was thin and distant. *This is no time to go frisking off! Where are you?*

I have no idea, she replied. *I think I took the wrong way out.*

Wait—I'll catch up, the boy ordered.

She looked at the iceless end of the valley. Where was Gold Ridge castle? For that matter, where were the farms and trees? If the land below had ever supported people, it did so no longer. Brush and reeds grew on the banks of the small river that trickled from the end of the ice-ribbon and lay more thickly on the sides of the valley, but it was all short growth, not very old. A herd of elk grazed in the distance as calmly as if it were full night. These animals weren't used to being hunted.

If she couldn't see the castle, she ought to know at least where Tris and Sandry were. She could certainly feel Briar's approach. Concentrating, she searched for a sign of the other two girls' magic.

There it was, miles away, and hidden behind a granite ridge. Their power was a glow on that horizon, shining through a layer of smoke.

The grassfires were closer to the castle than they'd been the day before.

That old buzzard Yarrun better do what he says he

94

can, Daja thought grimly. *I'd as soon* not *be grilled like sausage for a giant's supper.*

Where is *this place?* Briar demanded, popping from the hot springs to halt beside her. *You're* miles *from Gold Ridge!*

I know, she said. *Look at that!*

Briar disappeared so quickly she thought he'd evaporated like water in the sun. He'd jumped over to the icy ribbon and was drifting across its surface, visible just as a silver glimmer to her magical vision.

I don't want to go there, she told him. *It's cold. It won't like me!*

It's just ice, he protested.

And ice and smiths are supposed to mix? she demanded, ghosting down the cliff face. *I'll freeze and go all brittle and break.*

Have you ever seen anything like it? he asked, his voice filled with wonder. He seeped into a deep blue crack.

I liked the hot springs better, she said. The cold ate into her, making her feel sluggish and heavy.

There must have been something in her magical voice; he was at her side in a flash, urging her up the cliff face. The higher she rose, the more warmth she took from the stone. By the time they were at the ridge, she felt much better.

I saw a river down there, Briar remarked. *Melted water, running through a long tube in the ice. It was* beautiful! Recovering from his daze, he added, *What happened? We got in the hot springs under the castle and you were gone. We didn't wreck any plumbing, by the way. The water came through another crack in the stone. We should close the opening, though, before somebody gets flooded.*

How? Daja asked. *I don't know which of us did it or how, and I truly don't know how to stop it up again. Moving rock is what Tris does.*

Then let's ask her, the boy replied sternly. *Let's get it fixed and go back to work, before some long-neb finds our bodies just standing in the baths. You got your bond to her?*

Daja found it. Racing along, taking the quick way back to the castle and their bodies, they called to their friend. *Tris! Tris!*

*—and hematite to draw illness from a body—*Tris was memorizing one of the many lists Niko gave her while she worked. *To ground and stabilize, to focus on the physical plane, for scrying. Jade for love, healing—*

TRIS! Briar and Daja shouted, throwing their power behind the call.

What?! What? I'm busy! cried Tris.

Rather than waste time by telling her what had happened, they showed her images of the break in the ground Daja had made and the water jet shooting out of it. Tris needed a moment to sort out what they needed; the doubled images of the same event were more confusing than useful at first. *I'll fix it,* she told them grumpily. *And you better hope Niko doesn't find out.*

He won't if you stop jawing and get to it, Briar retorted, as he and Daja fell into their physical bodies again.

As they began to stretch limbs that had gone stiff, they felt Tris in the earth nearby, grumbling like a vexed housewife. By the time they walked out of the baths, she had used the bubbling force of the hot springs to block the channel Daja had opened.

"We'd better change clothes," Briar commented with a sigh. "If Lark sees us like this, she might think we got in a fight or something."

There was no arguing with that: all their work to get the mud out of their garments had just created large smears. Daja followed Briar to their rooms, where they changed into clean things. Daja also seized the opportunity to use their privy. On their way back to Lark, Tris, and Sandry, they peered into the courtyard where Daja's power had gotten away from her. Tris had done things properly. The only sign that hot water had jetted from the ground here was soaked earth and water-splattered stone.

*T*here you are," Lark began, rising to her feet when Briar and Daja returned. There was a look of welcome and relief in her eyes.

Daja blinked at the scene before her: she could see why Lark was so glad they were back. Across from the entry to the courtyard, someone had placed two piles of cushions on a groundcloth. Between the cushions was a low wooden table decked with covered plates, a pitcher, and a teapot. Little Bear lay with his muzzle on his forepaws, nose just touching the groundcloth, eyes locked on the plates.

In front of the whole arrangement waited Polyam. With a bow to Daja, the Trader indicated the cushions, and said, "It is a fine day for a conversation." The words were set by centuries of custom around the Pebbled Sea. They meant that the one who spoke them wished to do serious business.

Daja walked over, passing close to her forge. A quick glance into it showed that her white fire grid was gone, used up far below the ground.

"I beg you to accept this gift," Polyam added with a wave toward the iron vine. Beside it was a chased dish a foot in width. Daja picked it up. It was copper of a particular ruddy shade, with an inch-wide rim decorated in scalloped patterns, and a central design of shaggy horses and fur-capped riders in full gallop. It was a good piece of metal, comfortably solid in her hands. "It's just a token," commented Polyam, her words still those of bargaining custom. "To show my respect for your work."

Daja flipped the dish over, searching for the maker's mark. It was in one horse's round haunch; not the mark of a smith she knew. "This is Gold Ridge copper," she murmured. During the trip north, she had taken every chance to see and handle local metalwork. Long before their arrival, she knew the feel of Gold Ridge copper as well as she knew her own name.

"I bought it here," Polyam replied. "We come through every two years or so."

You must have done better then, to afford this, thought Daja. The plate was worth at least two silver astrels, a lot of money for a *wirok*. "I couldn't take one of your things."

Polyam shook her head. "I was a different woman then. The business I hope to do with you is more important."

Daja ran her fingers over the chasing. The copper sang behind her eyes as she stared at Polyam. At last she rested the piece next to the iron vine. Getting her staff from where it leaned against the wall, she laid it on the dropcloth and sat next to it, one pile of cushions at her back.

Once Polyam was seated with her own staff beside her, she carefully poured tea into small cups. Bargain-cups were supposed to be fine work; this pair had seen better days. Daja chose to ignore it. She had a feeling that Polyam had been forced to use her belongings—no one wanted the caravan's bargain-goods handled by a *trangshi*. They would only have to be cleansed later, or even destroyed.

Polyam raised her cup to Daja. "To business," she said.

Daja copied her. "To business." She sipped as her hostess did and hummed with pleasure. This was real Trader tea, hot, strong, flavored with smoke. She'd drunk nothing like it since her last night aboard Third Ship Kisubo.

Polyam smiled. "Talk needs food, or the talkers weaken." She took lids from the dishes, putting them aside. The plates were laden with things like cold vine leaves stuffed with rice, onion, garlic, and mint, tiny pickled onions, pastries filled with chicken or eggplant and spices, apricots stuffed with almond-rosewater paste, and small fruit tartlets. Last but not least, she saw almond and orange cakes. All were traditional foods among Traders, in caravans and ships alike, and Daja had not tasted any of them in months.

Looking at her knees, she bit down on her lower lip until she had beaten the urge to cry. If Polyam saw emotion, she would know that Daja was sensitive about Trader food, and she would have the advantage when they bargained. At last the girl took up the threadbare linen napkin Polyam had supplied and spread it over her crossed legs. "I really shouldn't," she said, as good manners dictated.

Polyam was very carefully staring at the table. "It is a poor effort, I know, but my mother's sister would be shamed to tears if I returned this uneaten."

Daja picked up one of each thing, arranging the food on her plate. When she finished her choices, Polyam followed suit. Carefully Daja lifted a tiny pickled onion to her lips and bit down, savoring the tart juice and the vegetable's crispness.

Little Bear whined. Daja glanced at him: he was still in the same position at the edge of the dropcloth, but his tail waved slowly. He whined again.

Something made her look past him. Briar and Tris watched her with nearly the same expression on their faces as the dog. Sandry was too well-behaved to be caught staring. Lark's back was to them as she helped Sandry to pull the sticks and threads of the new loom taut.

Daja looked at Briar and Tris again; her face twitched. Polyam twisted so she could see what was going on. Tris cut furiously at aloe leaves as the boy stirred bubbling seaweed.

"It would be *kaq's* manners not to share," Polyam muttered. "Will you join us?" she invited the others. Briar walked over immediately. Little Bear sat up, tail thumping.

"This is very kind of you," Lark said as she and Tris came to sit with them. Sandry joined them once she'd rolled up the loom.

"The people bargaining in Deadman's District never shared," admitted Briar, his mouth full of pastry. "They'd let us watch, though."

"Let us say I have a soft spot for dogs, then," replied Polyam, scratching Little Bear behind the ears. "And children."

"Your mother's sister must have enough *zirok* in Oti Bookkeeper's ledgers for the next three generations, if she cooks like this for a trade," said Daja. "Even my clan leader didn't cook so well."

"The head of your clan had to *cook?*" Tris wanted to know. "Why not make someone else do it?"

"Traders prize cooking as highly as the ability to negotiate better prices," said Lark. "That's why formal

102

bargaining includes gifts of food, isn't it, Polyam? People let down their guard if they're well-fed."

Polyam made a face. "It's not right that a *kaq* knows so much of *Tsaw'ha* ways," she muttered. To Daja she added, "Or that you are *teaching* them our ways."

"I was taught your ways by other Traders, when I was just a sprightly young thing," said Lark.

"She was an acrobat," Daja told Polyam.

"And a dancer," added Sandry.

"And she passed the tambourine for coins after they performed," Tris put in.

"I learned what I know traveling with my parents and my nurse," remarked Sandry.

"Then where are they now, your mother and father?" Polyam wanted to know, her eye bright with curiosity. "Would they be happy to see their child in the dirt, associating with commoners?"

"They're dead," Sandry replied flatly, tracing the embroidery on a cushion with her finger. "Both of them, in the smallpox epidemic in Hatar last fall."

"When the gods balance the books, mortals weep," Polyam said gravely. "I am sorry for your loss."

Sandry looked at her, small round chin thrust out stubbornly. "Besides, Uncle likes my friends. *And* he doesn't seem to mind dirt."

"Gods know we rode through enough of it these last two weeks," muttered Tris.

"What of you, boy?" Polyam asked Briar. "Where did you learn *Tsaw'ha* things?"

"In Hajra, in Sotat," replied the boy, taking another stuffed vine leaf.

"Don't look at me," Tris said hurriedly. "My family never associated with anyone other than fellow merchants."

"You all live in the same house, at a Living Circle temple city?" inquired the Trader.

The four nodded.

"And you are all *xurdin?*" she continued, using the word for mage.

"Niko found us," explained Sandry. "Niklaren Goldeye. Daja was shipwrecked, and he found her; I was hidden from a mob in a cellar in Hatar. Briar was being sentenced to—" She blinked, trying to remember her friend's one-time destination.

"The docks," he said. When Polyam looked at him, he showed her his X tattoos. "Caught thieving three times—but don't worry. Anyone that nicks Trader—*Tsaw'ha*—" he changed the word with a mocking grin—"things gets bad magic on them."

"And Tris was at another Living Circle temple," Sandry finished. She didn't add that Tris's family had given her away, being too frightened to keep her. Even now Tris hated to hear it mentioned. "Niko saw our magic, that no one else knew we had, and brought us to Lark and Rosethorn—"

"And Frostpine," interrupted Daja.

Sandry beamed at her. "I wasn't going to forget him. How could I? They had magic like ours," she told Polyam. "Well, and he brought me there partly because Duke Vedris is my great-uncle."

"It's quite a story," admitted Lark. "And it grows every day." She grinned. "Sometimes it's very tiring to be a part of it."

"Ack!" cried Briar. Now that the food was nearly gone, he realized his current pot of what he called "oil stew" might burn. Getting up, he ran over to tend it.

"So you were Blue Traders?" Polyam asked Daja.

Seeing Tris open her mouth to ask for an explanation of the term, Daja quickly said, "Those who travel the seas and rivers are Blue Traders. The ones who ride snow or sand are called White Traders." Answering Polyam, she added, "Blue Traders, on the Pebbled Sea."

"Speaking of snow, Polyam, didn't you come here from the north? How were the passes? Is autumn there as late as it is here?" Lark wanted to know.

Polyam refilled Daja's teacup. "Not in the Namornese Mountains," she replied. "But the closer we came to here, the more shrunken the snow and ice-fields on all but the highest mountains."

"Maybe you know what I saw," said Daja. "There was a river of ice, I swear it! In the higher mountains, about ten or fifteen miles—" She looked around, trying to guess directions from the sun. She pointed. "Southwest. It ended in a barren valley—"

"It looked more scraped than barren," Briar called from his table.

Polyam and Lark traded amused glances. "You have never seen a glacier before?" inquired the Trader.

"A glacier? A real one?" asked Tris, eager. "Where? Could I see it?"

"There is a small one, probably the one she means," Polyam replied. "The Dalburz—it flows out of the Feyzi ice cap in Gansar."

"But this looks like a river, except there are cracks in it," protested Daja.

"That's what a glacier is," Tris informed her. "A river of ice that grows and shrinks, depending on the weather. Lark, *please* can I see it?"

"We'll have to ask Niko," said the dedicate, getting to her feet and gracefully dusting off her behind. "Now, why don't we go back to work, so Daja and Polyam can bargain? Now that the ice is broken, so to speak," she added with an impish smile.

"Oh, all right," grumbled Tris, struggling to rise.

"Thank you for the blessing and the bounty of food," Lark told Polyam in Tradertalk, with a bow. She drew Tris away, translating what she'd just said. Sandry followed, after a small, polite curtsey to Polyam. Little Bear resettled himself, this time for a proper nap.

For a moment the Trader said nothing, twisting so she could look at Daja's friends as they settled to their tasks. When she turned back to Daja, there was no way for the girl to guess what thoughts were behind that scarred and yellow-marked face. "They say the ice caps from which the glaciers spring are miles deep," Polyam remarked. "I have a feeling that your story is much the same—I see only the tiniest part of what is there, for you and for all of them." She hesitated, then added, "When we have finished our bargain, I will add a packet of tea. I know it cannot be found."

The offer was a startling one. Their unique tea blend was one of the few things Traders did not include in business deals: while artisans, *lugsha*, might taste it in a bargaining session, they could not buy it.

At the mention of the reason they were there, both of them looked at the iron vine and the copper plate beside it. Daja gasped. Somehow, a rod in the trunk of the vine had separated from the others, to plunge one end into the plate. The metal around the iron looked soft and crumpled, as if the rod sucked the copper into the vine. On a branch near that rod and the plate, a tiny copper bud had appeared.

Daja got up and walked over to inspect her creation. Gently she turned it—and the plate—over. The thin piece of iron merged with the plate as if they were melted together, and copper striped the iron all the way back to the vine's trunk. Freeing the plate would be a chore, if it could be done at all. Ought she to ask Rosethorn for help?

"I'm *dreadfully* sorry," Daja told Polyam as the

Trader joined her. "I had no idea this would happen. None at all."

Polyam stared at plate and vine, rubbing her scarred ear. "Two gold majas," she said at last. "Even *gilav* Chandrisa won't argue, not when she sees this. And it seems I must find another token to give you, since I will be getting this one back in another form."

"Please," Daja said, putting a hand on the woman's arm. "A token isn't necessary."

Polyam's smile was wry. "First I am lectured in proper bargaining by your friends, then *you* tell me to ignore it. If we are to do this, let it be done correctly."

"Besides," Tris remarked from her seat near Briar, her gray eyes sharp behind her spectacles, "the more unusual *this* purchase is, the better *you* look to your caravan."

"That one could almost be *Tsaw'ha*," Polyam muttered.

Daja grinned. "Her family is a merchant house in Capchen," she explained.

"She's from *that* House Chandler? Then I should watch her." Polyam gave Daja a half-bow. "I must take my news back to the caravan, and find another token. Don't worry about the furnishings—someone will come for them. I have a feeling they won't expect me to clean up after this." With a nod to Lark and the other young people, she left the courtyard.

*   *   *

Soon after Polyam's departure, Lark called Daja, Briar, and Tris over. Sandry now sat cross-legged on the ground. Her loom was stretched out, anchored at one end by a strap around a table-leg and on the other by the strap around Sandry's waist.

"What we need to do," Lark explained, "is map the paths your magic has taken. Remember the thread you were given yesterday? Sandry will weave it here, calling a pattern from the threads themselves, rather than working her pattern out beforehand."

Briar fished the bobbin of silk from his pocket. It was grimy. "They're all the same color," he protested as Daja and Tris produced their bobbins. Daja's was dirtier than his, smutched with soot; Tris's was sticky with aloe sap. "How will she tell which is which?"

"Magic colors the threads as part of the spell," said Lark. "And there's something you should know. While she does this, Sandry will need your magic."

"All of it," added Sandry. "You won't be able to use any."

"For how long?" Tris wanted to know. She didn't like the idea of her power not being there if she needed it.

"For a day or so," replied Lark. "Once we see how the magics have mixed, Sandry has to separate them again so each of you will have your own power back, and completely under control."

Lark drew his bobbin from Briar's fingers. Daja

handed over hers. Tris had to think about it for a minute, before she too surrendered her thread.

Once Lark had all four bobbins, including Sandry's, she put them beside the backstrap loom and drew four new bobbins laden with thread from her pocket. "Carry these until we ask for them," she instructed, giving one to each of the four. "After Sandry maps the problem, she has to weave it right again. That's when we'll need fresh silk that's attuned to you."

The four young people tucked the new bobbins into their pockets. Sandry then gathered up the bobbins that Lark had put beside her. Taking the ends of all four threads, she twisted them together and began to wind them onto a shuttle.

"Lark, why aren't *you* doing this?" inquired Tris. "Is this the kind of thing a new weaver ought to be doing? No offense," she added to Sandry, who only grinned.

"Except that this particular new weaver has already spun magic, if you recall," said Lark. "I've never done such a thing. I can't manipulate someone else's power. And though I've woven maps on a loom, it's been for something physical—searching for the location of a lost child, once, or finding out where robbers had their lair. In tracing things of power, I would be helpless."

Daja, Briar, and Tris thought this over. Sandry continued to wind thread onto her shuttle.

Lark fiddled with a piece of scarlet thread, then continued. "The mages I've known either shape a physical thing to carry their power or they just wield magic as part of their own bodies. I can place a spell of invisibility in a cloak as I weave; Niko sees magic with his real eyes. Rosethorn's power grows with her plants. Frostpine builds in spells as he works metal. And most of the time that's how *you* all do magic—most of the time, but not always. We know Daja put magic onto iron so thoroughly that she changed its nature. Tris sprouts lightning—she doesn't need to wait for a storm. Sandry was able to spin a thing that did not exist in the physical world, your magics. Briar—"

"Me, I just cook things in the ground," said the boy glumly.

"Where did the fire to cook with come from?" Lark wanted to know. "Like Tris, you sprouted it." She hugged him around the shoulders with one arm and let him go. "We should have done this mapping weeks ago, the moment we knew that Sandry had combined your magics during the earthquake."

"But then the pirates came," said Tris.

Lark nodded. "And then we were cleaning up in Winding Circle and Summersea, and then the duke wished us to go north with him. Well, I don't believe we can put it off anymore. This may not be the best time or place, but it has to be done. Are you nearly ready?" she asked Sandry.

The girl nodded. Almost all of the thread from the bobbins was now wrapped around her shuttle.

Lark went to the archway. As the young people took seats near Sandry, Lark hooked one end of the crimson thread she'd been toying with on the right side of the arch. Her lips moved while she drew the rest of the thread across the opening, as if to bar it. Using her thumb, she pressed the free end of the thread to the opposite side, where it stuck. She put her palms together and rested her hands against her forehead, as if she prayed. To the eyes of the four, the archway thread began to glow, then burn with a fierce, white light. Lark sighed and returned to them, settling cross-legged onto the ground.

"That should spare us any interruptions. Now. Close your eyes," she ordered. The four obeyed. "As you meditate, pass a thread of your power to Sandry. She will add it to her weaving. Once you know she has it firmly in hand, you can go about your tasks."

"Is this going to hurt?" Tris wanted to know. "I'll hate it if it hurts."

"You'll feel a tug," replied Lark. "It shouldn't hurt."

I wish she hadn't said "shouldn't," Tris grumbled magically to the other three.

Oh, hush, Sandry retorted.

"Breathe in," commanded Lark.

Counting to seven as they inhaled, the four closed their eyes. Each time they did this exercise, it got easier to track their powers to their sources and to gather them up. Reaching into her magic, Daja obtained a pinch of it. Slowly and steadily she drew it as a wire, twirling it a bit to make it as thin as silk. Tris grabbed a miniature lightning bolt, one that trailed a cord that ended in the blaze of her power. Briar teased out a vine, the thinnest, most threadlike tendril. With her own power wound, one end trailing, around a bright thing that looked like a distaff at her center, Sandry waited for her friends to give her what she needed. She took Briar's first and joined it to her thread. Next came Daja's, then Tris's. Gently she twirled the four cords until they melted together to create a single length.

They felt Lark now as a shimmering presence that offered the shuttle to Sandry. As Sandry wound their power onto the shuttle, Daja, Briar, and Tris retreated into their own bodies and senses, coming out into the real world again. Even with their physical eyes open and all their senses returned, they felt the gentle tug as Sandry drew their magic away.

"Lakik's teeth, I'm burning!" growled Briar. He meant the pot of oil he'd left on the fire. He dashed to rescue it.

Daja built a new fire in her forge. Once it was burning nicely, she picked up five thin iron rods and set them to heat.

Tris returned to her pile of aloe leaves. When she lifted her knife, she saw her fingers were trembling. She didn't like the sensation of her magic being pulled from her one little bit. It startled her to realize how much she'd come to take that blaze of power inside her for granted. Not even half a year had gone by since she'd first grasped it; now she wanted it more than anything else in the world.

Gritting her teeth, she picked up a leaf and began to cut.

That evening, Lady Inoulia's big dining hall filled with talk of spreading grassfires, talk punctuated by coughs as occasional drifts of smoke came through the windows. All day long people had trickled into the castle, carrying their movable property in wagons or packs. While many were fed by an open air kitchen in the main courtyard, the important people, village headmen and artisans, dined with the castle residents. Sandry felt sorry for them and resentful, and was ashamed of her resentment. This summer she had seen too many refugees fleeing earthquake damage and pirate raids. She had hoped that, so far north, there would be no families driven from their homes.

She wished there was someone to talk with. On her left Lady Inoulia conversed with the duke. Niko, on her right, was speaking to Yarrun. Perhaps her friends . . .

Briar, Daja? she called silently. Nothing happened; they didn't even look up. Tris?

The redhead was chatting with the kitchen boy next to her. If she'd heard Sandry's mind-call, she gave no sign of it.

Frowning, Sandry touched the front of her dress, where the small pouch she wore on a chain around her neck lay hidden. The pouch held magical things, including a circle of thread with four lumps in it. It had been the first she'd ever spun, with a lump for each of them, a symbol of the way she had brought their magics together. With it under her fingers, she ought to have been able to speak to her friends.

Briar? Tris? Daja?

She felt no trace of magic, not in her call and not in the pouch. She was about to ask Niko what had gone wrong when she remembered the loom and her afternoon's work. If ever she needed proof that she had bound their power into her weaving, here it was. She didn't even have the thread circle's magic to use. With a sigh, she returned to her dinner.

"Is Tris well?" Niko asked Sandry a short time later. "She's coughing a great deal."

"It's the smoke," replied Sandry. "I wish there was a

way to screen it out. Has Uncle mentioned when we'll be moving on?"

"No, but I would guess not for another few days at least." Niko rubbed his eyes tiredly. "People from the smaller valleys along the Gansar border are expected to meet him here. We simply have to cope."

Once the meal was finished, the duke and Lady Inoulia stood. The lady held up her hands, motioning for quiet. "Men and you boys of the household who are older than twelve, report to Emmit Steward. It is necessary to dig a firebreak along the edges of the forest. He will give you proper instructions and tools."

People murmured anxiously. It was rare to create firebreaks—broad strips of bare ground that fire could not cross. Doing so now made everyone nervous.

"My friends, my friends!" Now it was Yarrun who motioned for quiet, one of his false-looking smiles plastered to his face. "You know me, as you knew my father before me. Have we ever failed you? This is a precaution, nothing more."

Sandry shook her head as she and Niko walked down to join Briar, Tris, and Daja. She would feel ever so much better if the person making such assurances were Niko, or Tris. It was hard to have faith in Yarrun. There was a lack of strength in his eyes, and his collection of humorless smiles made her skin crawl.

I hope Uncle isn't just getting advice from him about these fires, she thought, offering Tris her pocket handkerchief. The redhead took it with a relieved smile and used it to cover a burst of coughs.

Frostpine had not come to supper. It was only after Sandry had returned to work—hooking the free end of her backstrap loom to a cedar chest—that he arrived in their rooms freshly bathed. A servant came in his wake with a tray of food.

"I don't know *what* Tenth Caravan Idaram is doing," he told the children, Lark, Niko, and Rosethorn in between bites of chicken. "At first all they wanted us to do was touch up some metal work—replace a wheel, mend some harness. Then, this afternoon—*late* this afternoon—they say they want everything gone over. *Everything.* Every buckle, every brass stud, every ring or bit or clasp in the caravan. It's at least two more days work for Kahlib and me—his apprentice isn't good for much. I was so late because we had to make sure he has the raw metal for the work. He sent his apprentice to Owzun Manor for more brass. Of course Kahlib's happy as a"—he looked at Lark and grinned—"a lark. It's a fortune to him. I just thought the Traders wanted to clear out soon, for—for silly reasons of their own."

"Because there's a *trangshi* here," Daja remarked gloomily.

"But they changed their minds," Frostpine pointed out. "I think they want something so much it's *worth* being around a *trang—*"

He stopped. Briar had carried the iron vine over for him to see; Tris bore the attached copper plate. It was nearly half gone now, and the remainder was as buckled and rippled as if half melted. Now all the branches on the side of the vine closest to the plate sported copper buds.

"—*shi*," Frostpine said weakly. "Shurri defend us. They know about this?"

"That plate was Polyam's trade-token for me," Daja said. "We left it beside the vine. There was just one bud out when she left, but she raised the price to two gold majas when she saw it."

"Right there?" asked Frostpine. "She didn't ask to consult with her *gilav*?"

The four young people and Lark shook their heads.

"They have a buyer," Niko said firmly. "They must. It's the only reason to offer that much. They have someone who pays well for magical artifacts."

"Do you know who?" Rosethorn asked, inspecting the copper buds. It was the third going-over she'd given the vine since she'd seen it late that afternoon.

"There is a handful of people around the Pebbled Sea who pay highly for magical curiosities," replied Niko. "If you like, Daja, you might try to sell it directly to them."

Sandry looked at Niko, surprised. It was certainly Daja's right to try to go around Polyam, but it didn't seem honorable.

"No," Daja said, frowning. "I want them to think

Polyam dickered me exhausted and got an outrageously cheap price. That might replace some of the *zokin* she lost when they made her *qunsuanen*."

Niko smiled, approval in his dark eyes. Sandry glared at him. "Daja doesn't exactly need to be tested on whether she's honorable or not," she told him crossly.

"Doesn't she?" asked Niko. "Don't all of you?" He looked at each of the four. "This is your first taste of the things which may come from your being powerful mages. People will offer you gold, status, even love. I want to know how you will react. I want to know if your teachers will release greedy, thoughtless monsters into the world."

All four young people looked away.

"Well," Frostpine said cheerfully when the silence grew long enough to make Little Bear and Shriek stir restlessly, "while your creation was getting away from you, how did your ordinary work go? Let's see your nails, Daja."

With a groan, she fetched the bucket full of her afternoon's work. Smoke billowed in the window, making the others cough as she handed the bucket to Frostpine.

He said nothing at first, but the look on his face as he scooped up nails and let them run through his fingers was odd. "This makes no sense," he muttered. "Not in the lea— Where is it?" he demanded. "Where's your magic?"

"Sandry has it," replied Daja, startled that he'd asked.

"'Sandry has it,'" Frostpine repeated, eyebrows raised. "I see. You just, you felt generous, and you said, 'Take my magic, Sandry, I'm not using it—'"

"Don't get into one of your flames," Lark advised, tucking her hands in the sleeves of her habit.

"One of my—" Frostpine's voice rose. "You strip my apprentice of her power—"

"It's just a loan," Briar protested.

"Look at what Sandry's doing, before you say any-more," Lark told Frostpine.

He glanced at the young noble, who wove as she had since they returned from supper, deep in a trance of concentration. Working at a steady pace, she threw the shuttle, with its burden of power and silk thread, to and fro in the warp on the loom. Under her fingers lay three inches of cloth. Although the thread on the shuttle was creamy undyed silk, there was a pale touch of color in the cloth. On one edge a barely green stripe was shaping; on the other, an orange-red one. A white stripe lay inside the green one, while a blue tint brushed the cloth between the white and the orange. A second look showed that threads of each color trickled into the other stripes, starting just an inch away from the bottom of the loom.

"She's mapping, you great dolt," said Rosethorn sharply. "You know as well as we do that something must be done about the way their power is leaking.

Or do you want to put it off until lightning strikes whatever *you're* working on next?"

"You shouldn't encourage them to turn their power over to anyone," argued Frostpine, his eyes glittering with anger. "Not to each other, not to us, not to anyone on the face of the earth! *They* have no idea what evils could result, but I would have thought that *you* did!"

"We *do* know," replied Niko. "This must be done, and done now."

Daja rested a hand on her teacher's arm, not wanting him to be upset. "If you could feel my magic in plain work like nails, couldn't that be trouble someday?" she asked. "Lark thinks we can fix this now. I *want* it fixed."

"Me too," said Briar.

"Me three," added Tris.

Frostpine ran his fingers through his mane of hair. "I don't like it," he protested. "What if Sandry goes awry?"

"She can't," Lark replied calmly. "She and I bound every protective and enclosing spell I could think of into the warp and the structure of that loom before a single thread was woven. When she's done, loom and cloth alike will be taken apart and the thread burned."

Frostpine gave Sandry another look, then stalked out onto the balcony. Daja stared at the remaining adults. Frostpine never acted this way. Even during the pirate attack on Winding Circle he had stayed calm.

"I'll speak to him later," Niko said, rubbing his temples. "He's just miffed that we didn't consult him, even though he agreed that Lark and I make the decisions where this kind of learning is involved."

Daja wasn't sure that Niko was right. Frostpine didn't get into a swivet because he hadn't been asked.

"You know what I'd like to do tomorrow?" Tris announced. "I'd like to go see that Dalburz glacier. Could we?" she asked Lark and Niko. "I've never seen one."

"I have this to do," Sandry pointed out. It was time for a break. Sliding out of the loom, she walked around, rubbing the back of her neck.

"You should spend a few hours away from your loom in the morning," Lark told her. "You will be feeling today's magical effort. A ride will be just what you need to refresh yourself, and then you can work in the afternoon."

"I could guide you, if you wish to make the trip." Polyam stood in the open door, a package in her unscarred hand. She nodded to the adults in greeting. "Our caravan passes it all the time."

"I actually like the sound of this," Niko said with approval. "Tris should see a glacier, and the experience would be good for all of us. Lark and I will come, too."

"Well, if I'm to go riding in the morning, I'd best

get back to work now," Sandry commented with a sigh. Lifting up the backstrap, she stepped into it and sank to the floor, pulling her loom taut.

Polyam walked over for a better look at her cloth. "It's a mess," she said critically. "You were fine at the start, but your threads are getting all confused." Her frown crinkled the yellow-marked scars on her face. "And how can the stripes be colored? Your thread isn't."

"It's a long story," replied Lark, sitting with a basket of needlework. "Can we offer you something to drink?"

The Trader shook her head. "I came only to bring a new trade-token, since it looks as if I will buy my old one with the purchase of the main piece." She walked over to the iron piece, her staff thumping on the carpet. "It works fast, this vine."

"And it does so all by itself," Daja said. "It stopped drawing on my magic once Frostpine got it to let me go."

Polyam bowed, offering her the package she carried. "I hope you will take this as our new trade-token."

Her gift was wrapped in yellow silk, as were all important Trader gifts. Carefully Daja undid the knots. The cloth fell away to reveal a hand-sized figure of a long-tailed, spotted cat in palest green jade. Tris, Lark, and Briar gasped as Daja showed it to them. When the boy stretched out his hands, Daja let him take the figure. He examined it from all angles, running his fingers over the maker's mark carved in its base.

"It's called a snow leopard," Polyam explained. "Shy animals. They live in the southern mountains of Yanjing. They're actually white with black spots."

"Very nice," said Niko. "A worthy offering, don't you think, Daja?"

Daja nodded. "Yours?" she asked Polyam.

The Trader smiled. "No—it came from the caravan's goods," she replied, her good eye dancing.

"Then I will prize it," Daja replied, with a smile. She knew how such things worked. That she was offered a gift from the caravan's goods meant that she was rising in the opinion of the *gilav*. "You're still doing the bargaining, though, aren't you?" If they thought enough of what she had to sell that they would offer her a gift like this, they also might want a high-status *daka* bargaining, not Polyam. I don't want that, Daja realized. I like her. It was a startling thought.

Polyam shook her head. "They would have to *qunsuanen* the *dakas*. Why waste the time, and the paint"—she gestured to herself—"when I've gone through it already?"

Briar's lips moved as he did calculations. "I might get five silver astrels from a top-of-the-ladder pump for it," he said, handing the carving to Daja. "That means it's worth maybe a gold maja on the market."

Someone—Tris—gasped.

125

"I told *gilav* Chandrisa you'd probably sell at three gold majas," Polyam commented. "Don't make a fool of me." She smothered a yawn with one hand. "I'll meet you by the stables in the morning. For this, I believe I can even scrape together another bargaining meal." With a cheerful wave, she left them. Daja danced a jig, thinking of more Trader food.

"Polyam is enjoying this too much," said Niko sourly. "As are you four."

"We've been good all day," protested Briar. "We didn't use our magic without someone to watch us." Daja, standing behind him, saw his fingers cross behind his back. She agreed; if none of the castle's people had mentioned the appearance of a steam-vent in one of the courtyards, she and Briar weren't about to. "We've earned a bit of fun, don't you think?" Briar asked.

"I don't understand," Tris said, her voice hoarse. "At first she acted like she almost hated Daja, but now she goes to all this trouble, getting food and offering to ride with us—" She stopped, coughing.

"I think partly she does it because she can," Lark explained when Tris caught her breath. "Because they let her. As *wirok* she's a despised person. They give her their leavings—"

"And their scorn," said Rosethorn quietly. She had been seated at a desk, writing.

Lark nodded. "But now, she's the only avenue for them to buy something they want. She's getting

126

better food out of them than she might see for weeks, not to mention access to trade goods. They're listening to her now. I'd take advantage, in her shoes."

"I never thought of it like that," Tris admitted. She began to cough again. "It's all this smoke, from those grassfires!" she gasped. "I *hate* it."

"I don't like the sound of that," Rosethorn said. "Let me give you something for it."

"I don't want anything nasty," Tris croaked, following Rosethorn into the room where she and Lark slept. "I'll be all right."

Lark got out her needlework, keeping an eye on Sandry. Briar decided that Little Bear needed to be combed and set about it, while Niko picked up a book. Daja went onto the balcony.

Frostpine sat on the stone railing, his back against a section of wall. He glanced at Daja, nodded, then returned to staring at the valley below. Tris's starling, Shriek, was asleep on his shoulder, half tucked under some of the man's hair.

Daja sat nearby and looked at the view. The bands of fire were just a few miles from the lower edge of the forest. Drifts of smoke blew into her face off and on. They didn't affect her or Frostpine as they clearly did Tris and the others, perhaps because as smithmages they were used to smoke.

She wasn't sure what to say to him, so she said nothing. After a while she heard his quiet voice. "I was born in Mbau, southeast of the Pebbled Sea."

Hot country—good ebony, mahogany, and brass-work, though, Daja thought automatically. She remained silent.

"My father was a shepherd in our village. He was poor once. My older brother and sister talked about eating bean stew for days because that was all they had. There was enough money after I was born, though. My mother and sisters had several dresses. My father could pay someone to watch the flocks while he sat in the *shuq* with the elders, and told stories, and judged quarrels." There was a dreamy tone in Frostpine's voice, as if he told a story about someone else.

"Our *mchowni*—shaman, you'd call him—was like an honorary uncle. He ate with us on feast days, and brought us children presents. He found husbands for my sisters and a place among the warriors for my brother. I didn't like him. He was always watching me."

A larger-than-usual cloud of smoke drifted over the balcony. Taking a deep breath, Frostpine blew at it as if he were a bellows, driving it away. On and on his breath went, until no smoke remained in the air around them.

"I was 'the moody one.' Most of my time I spent with the blacksmith, fetching and carrying. When I was older, he taught me. I loved it, but it frustrated me, too. Something was missing. It was like always reaching for a tool, only to find it gone when you try to grab it. Some days I went so crazy that the only thing for it was to run, and run, and run."

He fell silent, his eyes closed. At last he continued, "When I was fifteen, the *mchowni* died. He died—and all of my magic, that he had taken and used since the day I was born, the magic he'd paid my parents for—it came back to me. I nearly died. It was like my veins were on fire.

"He didn't even know what kind of magic it was. He just used it to get what he needed. And me, the first time I walked into the smithy after I was well again? I heard all the metal singing. My tools melted when I picked them up. The smith ordered me out. My whole life was in ruins. And my parents told me it was for my own good. A blind man could see it was for *their* good that they sold my power."

"You never said," Daja whispered, her eyes stinging. She wanted to cry for the boy he had been.

"I was angry for a long, long time. I wanted to hate everyone. It took hard work for me to live past that anger, to realize how senseless it was. If I dwell on it, I start to get angry again, so I try not to dwell on it."

"What happened to you? What about your family?"

"I left. I had to—there was no one who could teach me, and I had to be taught. I still hear from my youngest sister. It took me a while to grow up enough to write to her."

"No wonder you were upset."

He sighed. "Lark is right—you four need this. The memories were just too much."

"It'll be over soon, I think," Daja reassured him. "When I get my magic back, I promise, I'll never give it up like that again."

Frostpine came over and kissed her forehead. "That's all I needed to hear," he said.

As they rode to see the glacier the next morning, Tris kept her fingers crossed that the journey would take them out from under the smoke that draped Gold Ridge for as far as they could see. She got a little relief from the cough that had plagued her all night as the road they followed led up, past the tiny crocus valley. Who would have thought such runty-looking plants would be worth so much? she thought as Briar pointed out the terrace where he'd fried some.

Sandry, her companion on the trail, was not her usual talkative self. The magical effort in her weaving had caught up with her as she slept, just as Lark had warned; she was pale and heavy-eyed, half-dozing in the saddle. Behind them came Niko, Yarrun, and Lark, talking idly. The Gold Ridge mage had offered to come along as far as the turnoff to the glacier valley: he wanted a look at the progress of the grassfires. At the rear of their column rode Briar, who had volunteered to keep an eye on the pack horse that carried their lunch.

Polyam, still decked out in bright yellow, and Daja led their company. Once Tris's starling, Shriek, had stopped filling her ears with his normal babble to hunt breakfast, Tris nudged her pony forward so that she could talk to them.

"A shame about the saffron crop," Polyam was telling Daja. "That's usually what we buy here. Lady Inoulia needs a miracle to get this valley through to the next harvest. They need rain, and they need copper and saffron. They're out of all three."

Tris looked soberly down into the valley. She could just see the edge of the shrunken lake far, far below: their road was carrying them to the river that fed it. "I wish I could *do* something," she muttered, thumping her leg with her fist. "Back home, I'd have it raining buckets!"

"Could you?" asked Polyam with a laugh. "Could you indeed?"

"She could," Daja said glumly. "And with as much thought as rolling over in bed."

Polyam's laughter died. "You're serious?"

Tris guided her pony to the outer edge of the

roadway. Their route sloped down now, into a wooded cleft where the small, grudging river that filled the lake entered Gold Ridge Valley. "Don't tell her what all I can do," she advised Daja. "It might just make her nervous."

"It might," Daja admitted. To Polyam she said, "Tris makes me nervous sometimes, and she's my *saati*."

Polyam shook her head. "To hear *kaqs* called *saati*—it makes me feel as if the world's coming all unglued."

"What else am I supposed to call them?" Daja asked, surprised. "Tris, Briar, Sandry—they're as close to me as my own blood. It's been a long summer," she said, wishing that explained their friendship and knowing it didn't even come close. "We've been through a lot together."

Yarrun rode up behind them. "You must excuse me for not going farther. I have no interest in glaciers," he announced. "Their power and mine do not mix. I leave you here." Clucking to his mount, he turned it toward the closer of the watchtowers that stood on either side of the river where it entered Gold Ridge.

"You might do better if you *did* have an interest," Tris muttered. "Whether your power includes them or not." Yarrun was starting to get on her nerves. He was so sure that everything he did was right and proper. After hearing Rosethorn, and after all the books she had read since beginning her magical education, she had to wonder. She *felt* the dryness in the valley below. It wasn't limited to the burning grasslands, the shrinking lake, or the shriveled fields. The ground everywhere was parched. She saw brown at the tips of leaves and needles on all the trees; looking at them made her itch.

That must be Briar's influence on her, she decided as they followed the river out of the main valley, bypassing the watchtowers. Throughout this trip she'd noticed she was more aware of plants and trees.

Looking ahead, she could see drying brush and grasses on the lesser valley's sides. Only the riverbanks were green. I've just been here a few days, she thought, wiping her forehead on her sleeve. How must it feel to have lived here for three years, with everything drying up?

Their party decided to eat midday a good distance from the glacier, after they discovered the wind that came off the towering wall of ice was *cold*. Looking around, they chose a broad stretch of sandy earth nearly a thousand yards away, atop a low, flat hillock at the foot of a cliff. Walking to the edge of their picnic ground while the food was set out, Daja stared up at the glacier.

Soaring over it in magical form the day before, she hadn't appreciated how vast the glacier was. She was impressed again by its noise: the thing filled the air with creaks, snaps, groans, and the babble of melting water. Listening, she began to think what she'd been told was true. The ice sounded as if it *did* move, however slowly. The long, steep gouges in the rocky walls of this valley could well be the marks of its claws as it shrank back from Gold Ridge.

"Daja," called Lark. She, Polyam, Briar—who liked to handle food if he couldn't stuff it into his mouth immediately—and Niko had placed everything neatly on a dropcloth. The meal looked like a king's feast, spiced with flavors Daja had known almost from the cradle. Now was the time to add *her* bit to the meal.

"It needs a centerpiece," she told her companions. Reaching into her saddlebag, she brought out her surprise and plunged it sharp end first through the middle of the dropcloth. There it gleamed in the sun, its inner petals just unfurling: a copper rose. "One of the buds was opening when I got up," she commented, pleased with the way everyone gaped in shock.

Kneeling, Briar stroked the flower. "I'll be switched," he muttered. "It's warm—I think it's still alive."

Polyam dropped to her good knee to examine the copper bloom. To Daja she said, "If you can learn to do this kind of magic on purpose, you'll be one rich *lugsha*."

Daja thought bitterly, I'd rather be a rich Trader, then shrugged. "First I have to learn how to do the magic on purpose, don't I?"

Once Lark spoke the blessing, no one talked—they were too busy eating—though each of them reached out from time to time to stroke the copper rose. The Trader food sweetened everyone's moods, once they'd devoured enough of it. The dessert pastries, thick with honey and nuts, made them all pleasantly lazy.

As Lark napped, Tris, Briar, Sandry, and Niko went for a closer look at the glacier. Polyam and Daja took a walk on the riverbank. Down here, close to the rampart of ice, the water was deeper and swifter. In the shade the air was cold; they kept to the sun.

For a while they said nothing. Then Polyam misjudged a spot where she stepped with her wooden peg, and the sandy ground crumbled away. She windmilled, almost going into the water. Daja grabbed her, dragging her back.

"I'm *fine*," Polyam growled the moment she was steady.

Understanding, Daja stepped away. She didn't want anyone to think *she* ever needed help and support, either. "You ride well," she remarked, thinking that might help her companion to feel less helpless.

Polyam snorted. "For short distances, like today," she replied, rubbing the thigh muscles of her bad leg.

Daja made a face. She'd wanted to make the woman feel better. Instead she'd reminded her of another thing she couldn't do easily, yet another thing that White Traders, at least, needed to be good at.

To her surprise, Polyam admitted, "I cramp up. It's

better to walk for long trips, even when the footing isn't so good."

Daja couldn't help it—the words were out of her mouth before she could stop them. "What happened to you? How did all this—" She gulped. "I'm sorry. It was rude of me to ask. It's none of my business."

Polyam stared into the heat-rippled air that rose from the cliffs across the river. "I used to be the best handler of horses, mules, and camels in Tenth Caravan Idaram," she said dreamily, clearly thinking of better days. "The best in all Idaram caravans. About twenty months ago, we were crossing the Osar Mountains, in Karang. It's bad country there, very bad. A rockslide covered the road, and I was trying to get our string of horses across, leading them myself. The rock shifted. I went down, and kept sliding, all on my side. It was shale—nasty rock that breaks up into sharp pieces. It carved my leg to the bone, took my eye—my whole left side looks just like my face." She touched the thick scars on her cheek.

"Trader and Bookkeeper," Daja whispered. "Your healers couldn't help?"

"They're healers, not gods," Polyam told her. "I was no good with horses after that. You know we like to carry only half-broken animals, so their owners can train them as they like. Without two good legs to balance on, I tried, but—"

"I'm sorry," Daja said.

137

"You're sorry for *me?*" Polyam's smile was twisted. "At least *I'm* still *Tsaw'ha.*"

"Is being *wirok* so much better than being *trangshi?*"

Polyam stared at her as if she'd run mad. "What a silly question! Of course it is! Of course!" She ran her fingers over the cap on her staff, as if memorizing the engravings and inlays that told her life story. "I'll pray to Koma and Oti every day that you find a way to lay up so much *zokin* that your name will be taken from the *trangshi* logs, and you'll be able to return to our people again."

Watching Polyam's fingers glide over her staff's etched metal cap, Daja used a hand to cover the top of her own staff, hiding its unmarked brass from view. "Is there that much *zokin* in the world?" she asked wearily.

"It's happened before," said Polyam. "It could happen again. I feel sorry for the ship or caravan that would owe you that much, but at least you'd be among your own. That's what matters." She looked at Daja and said sharply, "Wouldn't you *want* to return to the *Tsaw'ha?*"

Daja kicked the dry and sandy earth at her feet. "Yes, of course," she said automatically. "But you can't be *Tsaw'ha* and *lugsha*, not ever."

Polyam blinked. "If you were *Tsaw'ha*, why would you want to be *lugsha?* There'd be no point to—"

"Daja!" someone yelled. Looking up, Daja saw Tris

racing toward them, plump legs thumping the ground. "Daja, c'mere!"

"They're all right, for *kaqs*," Polyam remarked quietly. "But you can't turn ashes to gold, and you can't turn *kaqs* into real people."

Tris halted before them, gasping for breath. "Daja, didn't you hear me calling? Why didn't you come?"

Daja glared at her. "We were *talking*," she said, annoyed. What made Tris think people had to drop everything the moment she bellowed?

"But this is *important*," insisted the redhead. "Now look. You said you came up near here through hot springs, right? Do you know where? Is it near this place? Briar can't remember."

Tris and her questions. Did she ever stop asking them? Trader children, as Daja knew quite well, spoke when they were spoken to.

"*Daja . . .*"

There would be no shutting her up until she was satisfied. Squinting her eyes against the glare, Daja scanned the rising dirt and rock on their side of the river. A few hundred feet up, she found the green line of ridge. A white shaggy face, long and solemn, topped by small black spikes of horns, stared down at the people below. "About fifty feet back from where that grandfather goat is, the ground rises again. Over that rise are the hot springs."

Niko, Sandry, and Briar, walking at a more sensible pace, caught up with them.

"If we had our magic, we could go into the ground under the springs and see if the cracks continue on under the ice," Tris remarked to Niko.

"I'm *sorry* you don't have your magic," commented Sandry defensively.

Niko patted her shoulder. "It's all right—we couldn't have put the mapping project off, not the way the magics were breaking out. Everyone knows you worked to exhaustion yesterday."

Sandry stuck her tongue out at Tris, who only grinned.

Niko continued, "See those giant pieces of rock jammed together, the line they form?" Everyone stared at the slabs of granite that lined the valley walls on their side of the river. The stones looked as if a powerful force had shoved them together until one piece slid up another. "Those show that two sections of the earth are pushing together here. They run through this part of the valley."

"I don't understand," complained Daja, leaning on her staff. "What's so important about the hot springs and stone cracks?"

"Water," said Briar. He'd removed his shoes. Sitting on a rock, he lowered his feet into the river—and yanked them out with a yelp. "That's *cold!*"

"Ice melt," Polyam reminded him, grinning.

"Water," Tris said irritably, seeing that Daja still had not figured out what she was driving at. "How do we get more water into this river, and into Gold Ridge

Valley, when we've tons of the frozen stuff right here? See, with hot springs nearby, it means that lava's close to the surface—"

"Or that it's easier to reach," Niko said. "If the lava gets into faults in the earth that go under where the glacier is at its thickest, we can get the ice to melt faster."

Now Daja saw it. "It'll run downstream to the lake. Gold Ridge will have water."

"Niko says parts of the glacier are thousands of feet thick," Tris explained. "That's *maybe* enough weight to keep the lava from bursting through. That'd make a volcano, which we *really* don't want."

"Don't forget we also need caution with regard to how much ice melts," Niko pointed out. "Too much heat, and you run the danger of flooding, or mud slides."

Polyam looked at them oddly, her good eye shuttling nervously from face to face. "You talk about using the power of the earth as *you* might a hammer that lay near your hand," she said, looking at Daja.

"It's what they do," Niko told her quietly.

"And Daj' might never have found out she could," Briar reminded them. Gingerly he put his feet back in the water, a little at a time. "The way you people are about tools and making things, she never would have gotten near a smithy."

Daja didn't want to hear that, from him or from anyone. She turned away.

"If there's a way to get more water to Gold Ridge, Lady Inoulia should be told," Sandry remarked with a yawn. "She needs all the good news she can get right now."

"I thought you didn't like her," Niko said, his eyes amused.

"I don't," admitted Sandry. "But her people are nice enough, and they'll benefit from anything we can do."

With that, all of them returned to collect their things. Topping the hillock where they had eaten, they halted. Lark knelt on the dropcloth, as if she'd gone to retrieve Daja's copper flower as she cleaned up. Now she waved them closer.

The flower had grown. The stem Daja had thrust into the ground was thicker; two more stems sprouted from the earth around it. All three had split into lesser branches and leaves. A bud was already forming at the end of the middle stem.

Daja fell to her knees beside Lark. Reaching out, she cupped her original blossom in her hands, and gently felt the petals. They were the same thickness they had been when she put the flower down for a centerpiece. Unlike the iron vine, the flower hadn't lost metal in its race to put out more shoots. The rest of the new plant was sturdy.

"I don't understand," she complained, looking up at Niko. "There's maybe four times the copper here than was in the flower I brought from the castle. It can't just make copper from air!"

"Where do plants get what they need to grow?" asked Briar, his face eager.

"From the ground," Sandry murmured. "They get it from the ground."

"But the ground's just *dirt*," protested Tris.

Daja could hardly breathe, she was so excited. "Except when it has metals in it," she told the redhead. "It's getting the copper it needs to grow from—"

"More copper?" whispered Tris.

"A *lot* more copper," Daja said with a grin.

"Are you *sure*?" demanded Polyam.

Frustrated, Daja rocked back on her heels. "If I had my magic, I could follow it down and *be* sure!"

"I am sure," said Niko, getting to his feet. "This thing has found a vein of copper to take root in."

"Lady Inoulia should be notified right away," Lark pointed out. "No doubt she'll want to send soldiers to hold this ground. And maybe one of us should stand guard while the others return, to guard the copper plant from any of the local ruffians."

"That won't be necessary." Niko stepped to the edge of the dropcloth, and took a deep breath. Lark drew or motioned everyone away from the copper plant.

"What's he doing?" Polyam whispered to the others.

It was Tris, Niko's student, who answered. "His magic has to do with seeing things, all kinds of things. He's going to change how people see what's on this spot."

"Hush," Niko ordered without opening his eyes. Pressing his hands together, he bowed his head. White fire streamed across the space between him and the copper plant. Sinking to the ground, it wrapped itself around the metal, forming a cylinder that built until it was nearly five feet tall. Branches thrust out from it, and sprouted twigs and leaves. The white fire grew dim, replaced by brown or green color. At last Niko dropped his hands, and opened his eyes. His perfect tree illusion solidified and settled.

"Very nice," said Briar with approval. "Couldn't have done better myself—"

"Couldn't do it at *all* yourself," muttered Tris.

Briar ignored her. "But you'd never find a cork oak in these parts. Too cold."

Niko looked down his nose at the boy. "I beg your pardon?"

Briar shrugged. "Just thought I'd mention it."

Niko glared. The tree-shape rippled, and became a long-needled pine sapling. "All *right*?" he demanded, stalking over to gather his saddle and bridle. "If we are done picking at nits, I would like to return to Gold Ridge!"

Grinning, Briar went to saddle his own mount.

By the time they approached the cut where the river entered Gold Ridge Valley, they could see that the smoke lay even thicker there than it had before. Tris retreated behind a damp handkerchief tied over her

144

nose and mouth. Soon everyone but Daja chose the same kind of protection. Nothing kept the smoke from stinging their eyes, and all of their horses made it clear they did *not* appreciate riding toward the smell of fire.

Polyam slipped between Daja and Tris, the worst riders, to help them control their ponies. "What price for your vine?" she asked Daja, wet cloth muffling her words as they rode between the twin watchtowers. "Tenth Caravan Idaram will be here one more day, but then we must go. Frankly, if you will excuse the play on words, things are getting a little too hot around here."

Tris groaned and coughed.

"I thought, two gold majas," replied Daja soberly, looking up at Polyam. "That would increase your *zokin* even more, since you told them you thought I'd sell at three."

"What kind of *Tsaw'ha* are you?" demanded Polyam. "This isn't about my *zokin*, but your profit! You know as well as I that *gilav* Chandrisa thinks she can get at least six gold majas in a sale."

"I don't need a lot of money right now," said Daja with a shrug. "You people will want to buy from me again, yes? When I know what I'm doing and I create things because that's what I *want* to make, not because I had an accident, then I'll charge more. It doesn't feel right to get rich off something that's a mistake."

Sandry took pity on Polyam, who stared at Daja slack-jawed. "Why not pay two gold majas and three gold astrels?" the noble suggested. "That's over half a maja more—they'll think you bargained until Daja was addled, to get her to sell at a price like that."

Daja grinned at Polyam. "She's right, you know. Your *zokin* will be higher than ever. You'll be known as the hardest-trading *wirok* north of the Pebbled Sea."

On and on they debated as they passed from the smaller valley into the larger one. Looking across the river, Lark cried out in dismay.

A hundred yards downslope from the far watchtower, an almond orchard was in danger of fire. Its only barrier was a fringe of dry, open grass just thirty feet wide. A band of low, hungry flames was gnawing on that. Already sparks and stems of burning grass were drifting into the trees.

Lark fumbled for her saddlebags, muttering. Niko stopped her with a soft word as Yarrun rode out from under the trees, onto the grass. Halting his mount, he threw his fire-stopping powder into the air. His horse, it seemed, was used to such antics and remained stock-still, only twitching its ears as the powder drifted past.

Speaking that unfamiliar language, Yarrun shaped signs with his fingers, just as he had their first night in the valley. Once again the fire went out. The mage slumped in his saddle, bent over the horn.

Lark started to urge her mount to the bridge, to see if he was all right, but he straightened and shook his head at her. Fumbling in his saddlebag, he drew out a flask and removed the cap. He held it up as if toasting Niko.

"I have my uses, don't I?" he cried, his voice harsh. "At least I'm important for half the year! They wouldn't give me a teaching position at Lightsbridge, no, but here no one could manage without me!"

Shivering, Lark turned her mount and urged it up the road to the castle. Silently, the rest of the small company followed. Niko came last this time, looking back often at that lone figure on the riverbank.

The only one who enjoyed the rest of the ride was Briar, and he felt restless. Passing the saffron terraces, they caught a glimpse of Rosethorn, laboring with a handful of farmers in the many pockets of soil. Briar growled, seeing her there without him. He wanted his magic back; he wanted it *fixed*.

Since that was out of his hands, and he knew it would hurt Sandry if he complained, he tried to put it out of his mind. He succeeded for the most part, though every now and then the picture of Rosethorn barefoot in sandy earth returned to itch him.

Once their group reached the castle, it broke up.

Niko went in search of Lady Inoulia to discuss matters like glacier water and a new copper mine. Polyam returned to her caravan to report the result of her efforts. At last it was only Lark and the four young mages in the rooms they'd been given. Little Bear was there to greet them, out of his mind with joy after having been left behind. It took them a while to calm him down.

Once everyone was seated, Sandry brought out the rolled up backstrap loom. Hooking one end around a table leg, she stretched out the length of woven threads, straightening the edges until each fiber lay completely flat. Briar soon found he didn't want to look at the thing. Its ghostly colors shifted under his eyes, as if he viewed the work through a heat haze. Little Bear sniffed it and jumped halfway across the room with a yelp. After that, he kept his distance.

Sandry looked at her work, rubbed her eyes, and looked again. "Lark?"

"We need to do one more thing to make it stable," the dedicate said. She opened the leather pouch she took wherever she went and drew out a long, thin vial. From it she poured a mound of colorful dust into one hand.

"What is it?" Tris wanted to know. "What's it for?"

Lark smiled. "It's powdered flint, hematite, angelica, star anise, and lotus," she replied. "When I need to see magic in my cloth, see it as Niko does, this is what

I add to the fabric. It should help us sort out the map that Sandry has made."

She knelt beside the weaving and motioned for Sandry to do the same. "Hold out your hands," she instructed. When Sandry obeyed, Lark poured the powder into the girl's cupped palms, asking, "Can you feel your power in the weaving?" Sandry nodded. "Call it into the dust," Lark instructed. "Then sprinkle the dust on the cloth. Try to cover every speck of woven material. I'll be inside the working with you, but just as your guide. All right?"

Sandry closed her eyes and nodded.

The powder blazed: Briar, Daja, and Tris covered their eyes. Little Bear fled into a bedchamber. It was impossible to see what Lark and Sandry did, but the others *felt* it. Tris's teeth ached. Briar's nose was running; he groped for a handkerchief. A fierce ache spread from Daja's stomach to her bowels. She curled up, clutching her belly. They all heard Sandry cough thinly.

The pain and pressure stopped. The light faded.

"Ow," Daja said weakly, straightening.

Briar lurched to his feet, blowing his nose.

"Excuse me," Lark said weakly. She ran into their privy. From the sound, she made it just in time as her lunch came up.

Sandry tried to stand and fell against the table. She clung to it in a panic as she struggled to keep her knees from buckling and throwing her onto her work.

Just then she would have been quite happy never to look at that weaving again. She was certain the warp threads had been replaced by her veins, the weft threads by every fiber in her muscles. She hazarded a look at Tris. The redhead had not taken her hands from her eyes.

"Tris," she croaked. "It's all right."

"Tell me you didn't know it would be that bad," was the whispered reply.

"I had no idea it would—it would have so much kick." That was Lark, using the door frame to brace herself. She finished wiping her face with a wet hand-kerchief. "It's *never* been so violent before." She cleared her throat. "The difference is you four. You were strong to begin with. Then you were spun to-gether, and made stronger. Now you are all tangled, so the effect is—expanded." She gestured weakly at the loom. "If we can *un*tangle you, things should be more manageable."

Sandry wiped her face on her sleeve and looked at the thing she'd made. Now the colors were so dark it was impossible to believe that she had used undyed thread. She could also see clearly what had become of their magic. For an inch or so her stripes were clear and even, as straight as if drawn with a ruler. Past that one-inch mark, hair-fine fibers strayed, first across the borders between stripes, then further. By the point where she had four or five inches of cloth, the colors were hopelessly scrambled as green, orange, white, and blue formed a satiny layer over the warp threads. Putting her nose to the cloth, she tried to pick through that smooth coat to see its underpinnings, without success. She would have to respin the silk to make it form individual threads again.

"This explains more than it doesn't," Lark commented. "And separating your powers after this will take days. You'll start with your fresh silks. Each time a fiber splits off, you'll have to stop and force it back into its proper thread."

"We'd be like we were at the beginning of the summer?" Tris inquired. "Me all weather magic, Sandry all thread magic—"

"I don't like having lightning pop out of me," Briar said, "but this mix-up isn't *all* bad. It's fun seeing magic, like we caught from Tris—"

"I like weaving fire," pointed out Daja. "I made a lamp for myself that way, when I was in Kahlib's smithy, and the square I made yesterday turned out useful, too."

"Would we stop talking mind-to-mind, like we do now?" Tris asked. "That started after Sandry spun our magics together in the quake."

"I don't know," Lark admitted.

"And this living metal thing is *useful*," argued Briar. "Look how much the Traders will pay for the iron vine. We found that copper because of it."

"But something *has* to be done," Lark reminded

them. "There has to be some control of your power. You know there does."

"What if I just separate this mess into stripes again, and keep the fibers from escaping the threads?" inquired Sandry. "I could put a border on each stripe from here on. Our magic will still be mixed, but if each stripe is enclosed—"

"You'll be able to grip your powers," Lark murmured, running her fingers through her glossy curls as she paced. "They won't stray from your control." She looked at the weaving, and sighed. "I certainly can't be sure that we'd succeed in pulling your magics apart, or that they would stay separate—not without the border you suggested. And why didn't I think of a border for each stripe?" she asked her student, her eyes dancing. "Some master I am!"

"You would have thought of it," Sandry protested. "Maybe I'm interwoven with you." She grinned impishly at Lark.

"I'll discuss this with your teachers," Lark told the other three. "If they agree, Sandry could disentangle you tonight, before we go to bed. In fact, I think I'll go down to the village and talk to Frostpine right now."

"I'll find Niko," volunteered Tris.

"Do all of you still have those bobbins of thread I gave you?" Lark wanted to know. All four young people dug into various pockets and produced them.

"Very good. Keep them with you." The woman looked at the loom. "Let's put this away for now. The emanations are making my teeth hurt."

"E-ma-na-tions." Briar sounded the word out. "That's feelings, right? It's giving off magical feelings."

"Right," said Lark, tweaking his nose. "We'll make a scholar of you yet."

Sandry knelt beside her work and cautiously began to roll it up.

Daja was restless. Part of the afternoon was left, but there was no time to start the forge and get any real work done. After prowling the castle for an hour, she returned to their rooms to get a file and the nails she'd completed the day before; at least she could sharpen the points. She actually managed to do a dozen or so before the chore became unbearable. She threw the file across her bedchamber and stomped out again, ignoring Briar and Tris as they looked up from making more burn ointment.

The sight of them carefully straining oil from aloe lent more fuel to Daja's temper. Didn't they realize it was make-work? Yarrun wasn't about to let any fires break out of control!

What she wanted—what she couldn't have—was the sea. She ought to be there now, at a ship's rail with the wind in her face, breathing in clean salt air as her vessel leaped forward. How had she gotten trapped in this stupid mountain valley? If she couldn't be *Tsaw'ha*, at least she could be home in Winding Circle, where she could stand on the wall and breathe in that wonderful ocean scent.

The wall here would probably smell of fire. Well, that would have to do. Fire at least was her friend, and helped her to do the only important thing the *Tsaw'ha* hadn't taken from her. Her mind made up, Daja went looking for the way onto the castle's outer wall.

"If it's seeing you want, why not try the lookout tower?" offered a manservant when she asked for directions. "There's someone up there now, watching the fires, but they don't mind visitors."

Hoping the lookout wouldn't be in a mood for conversation, Daja followed the man's instructions. There were guards by the door at the base of the tower, but they let her pass without asking her business. She climbed, and climbed, and climbed. Just when she thought that if she climbed any more she would get a nosebleed, she reached the end of the stairs. The door at the top stood open—when she walked through, she stood by a tiny kiosk at the center of a broad platform. Its edges were guarded by a battlement as high as her chest. Made of stone, the battlement was pierced with holes to let the wind pass through. At this height, the wind blew hard.

It vexed her to realize she was nervous about approaching the edge. Hadn't she done crow's-nest duty a hundred times on Third Ship Kisubo? She ventured a step from the door, and another. The deck—the floor—was reassuringly firm under her feet.

"It's not so bad." Yarrun walked over from the far side of the platform. The wind clawed at his tunic and shirt; his hair was tumbled. "And it's stood for a century." He drank deeply from a flask in his hand.

Daja frowned—was he drinking liquor? The last thing *anyone* needed was a tipsy fire-mage. It was not her place to correct an elder, but with so much in the valley dependent on this one man, the thought of him as a drunkard was not a comforting one.

Her fear of the height evaporated. She walked to the battlement and took in the view. They were above the entire valley, except for the surrounding mountains. The ground was a quilt, its patches sewn from orchards, fields, villages, and pastures. The much-shrunken lake was a puddle in the quilt's center. Black stripes were laid across the neat squares, showing where grassfires had burned without regard for order. More such stripes blazed orange or glowed orange-black. The threat was still very much present, particularly in the grasslands nearest the castle. Just below, in the northern third of the valley and on each side, moss-green belts of forest grew on land too steep to be farmed. Over everything drifted a pale gray haze of smoke.

"All the locals talk of is the wealth in copper and saffron." Yarrun had come to stand next to her. "Those trees—they're wealth, too, in wood and resin and nuts. They could live on such wealth, if they had to. And that woman tells me to let it burn!"

"Rosethorn does know plants," Daja said cautiously. "That's her magic."

"Magic!" he scoffed. "Magic cannot take the place of *learning*, girl. This mumbling of earth rhythms and of nature is folly. True learning is gained when other people can work their spells as you do and get the same results. And you *need* learning to properly understand how the world functions. If you rely only on intuition or magic to interpret what you observe, you will think that animals truly are wise, not that they've learned if they do a thing it will please you. You will believe that only the proper ceremonies will ensure that the sun rises every day, as the people of the Kurchal Empire once did." Lifting his bottle, he drank deep.

Daja glanced at it sidelong.

He saw and raised the flask. "I would offer you some, but it wouldn't be good for you. This is a strong-brewed Yanjing tea, black as coal and treated with stimulants like foxglove. Called as I am this year to work day and night, I find that my tea helps me to keep going."

"It's not liquor?" she asked, suspicious.

"Spirits would be fatal. They destroy concentration and reflexes."

At least that made sense. She leaned on the railing and stared at the valley in silence. Yarrun, too, was quiet, letting his eyes roam from east to west. She peeked at him once and noticed that he trembled slightly. His stimulants? she wondered, then shrugged the question off and turned her face into the wind.

The sun inched its way down the sky, bound for the mountains. Already in the west a rim of shadow draped itself over the toy figures of the twin watch-towers and the cut that led to the glacier valley. She could see the specks that were Rosethorn and other workers on their way out of the saffron terraces. On the forest's edges the boys and men who bared strips of earth to serve as firebreaks chopped and dug, trying to expand the gap between the oncoming grassfires and the trees.

Yarrun was restless. He walked to the far side of the platform, but stayed only a few minutes before he returned.

"Can I ask something?" Daja inquired. The worst he could do would be to order her off the platform.

"Ask what you please," he replied absently, staring at the firebreaks. "I can't promise to answer, of course."

Adults! Why were they always so complicated? Daja made a face. Since his back was to her, Yarrun didn't see it. "Why did you say that to Niko, the first night we were here?" she inquired. "That he could do nothing to stop the fires? What did he do to you?"

The man took another turn around the platform, strolling all the way around its rim. He was quiet for so long that she believed he wouldn't answer. She was thinking perhaps she ought to go inside when Yarrun said, "You are young. Young, and gifted with unusual magics. You are to be congratulated."

Congratulated? Daja thought of Briar, grieving over burned crocus bulbs in private. What about Tris, who woke screaming three nights in four with dreams of slaves drowned when she had turned lightning on the ships they rowed? Or Sandry, who carried a rock spelled to hold light with her all the time, because she was terrified of the dark? What about Daja herself, *trangshi* forever?

With no idea of the thoughts that raced through her mind, Yarrun continued, "People like you and Niklaren Goldeye will never be just another mage. You will never work day in and day out at ordinary spells—never mind that our world cannot do without spells to keep food from spoilage, or spells to hunt down criminals. Ordinary mages live in shabby rooms. They scramble for money to pay for rent and supplies. And the *moment* someone like Goldeye comes to town, no one has time for you anymore. You aren't as interesting as he is—you aren't as famous. You just do the spells to ward off pickpockets, and keep plumbing and chimneys from clogging."

She was sorry she had asked.

Yarrun wasn't done. "I worked for twenty years after I left the university, traveling constantly, trying to become one of the great ones. Why not? I was good. It was simply a matter of finding the right spells, and the right patron. Every time my father wrote, it was 'When you stop deluding yourself and want a *real* job, come home.' Finally, I did. I came home, to put out fires in north Emelan. And here I am, working magic few others have the talent for, while my lady seats Niklaren Goldeye at the uppermost table, and me with him. My *usual* place, when no great mages visit, is just above the salt, with the chamberlain and the steward." He drank from his flask and smiled bitterly. "Now you regret that you asked."

"Not at all," Daja lied firmly.

Yarrun upended the bottle—only a few drops fell to the platform. "I must refill this. Were I you, I would pray that no one comes to think smith-magic is ordinary, or you will learn to your sorrow I am right." He left her there and went inside.

Daja nibbled a thumbnail. Wasn't it foolish, to worry over fame? Was it useful, to fret about someone else's magic? It was a thing you had or you didn't, whatever Yarrun believed about learning just the right spells. And she would give it all up in a breath, to be *Tsaw'ha* again.

Turning her face into the smoky breeze, she let it blow Yarrun's bile from her mind.

Sandry wove.

At first she knew what happened around her: Briar and Tris made ointment, Daja left and Lark returned.

160

Someone fed Little Bear; she smelled the food. Shriek sat on the pole at the far end of the loom and chattered; when she didn't feed him, the starling left. At last everything faded as she continued to work. She felt like a glass filled with light. Under her fingers the pattern wriggled, as if made of worms. Those were the magics, spilling out of control. They fought her grasp as she wove, but she refused to release them. They had run wild since the month of Mead: playtime was over.

What had happened? In one terrified moment, positive the stones around them would grind her, her friends, and their dog into paste, she had remembered her spinning lessons. It had made sense right then to gather the threads of their power and spin them together to make them stronger, to give them a way to fight the quake. And just look how things had turned out!

She had done this. It was only right that *she* set the magics right.

Here was Briar's new thread, wound onto its own shuttle, not twined with the others as the first threads had been. He was anchored in the satiny mess on the left side of the cloth, in the area that had started out as his. Taking up the shuttle, Sandry concentrated on him. These days he smelled wonderfully of damp earth and herbs, of aloe, pine trees, and a tumble of flowers. Here a loop of silk caught his quick hands as he slipped a roll into his shirt-front, or balanced a knife on a fingertip. A shift of the light and she had his pale gray-green eyes under thin black brows. A ghostly hand tugged one of her braids, his favorite trick when she wasn't looking. She reached the end of his stripe.

Now the border, a plain white cotton thread on a tiny shuttle, an empty piece with nothing of anyone in it. In her mind it was a glass wall, keeping Briar to one side, Tris to the other. Ten warp threads later, she let that shuttle go and picked up the next, the one that held Tris's thread. It too was white, but silk like Briar's, with a moonglow shimmer to it. Now Sandry had to forget the boy for the moment and concentrate on Tris.

Tris was easy to call to mind. This strand was coarse red hair, its curls scissored off, banished until Tris no longer grew lightning bolts in it when she lost her temper. Here was the smell of old books, and a hint of wood polish—Tris liked housework. Here were storm-gray eyes, gentling as Tris combed Little Bear's coat, when she thought no one else saw how much she loved their ungainly dog.

Too quickly Sandry reached the end of Tris's stripe. Well, she would return in a moment. Picking up another small shuttle, Sandry closed the redhead in with a fresh white border.

Now she had come to her own stripe. What was she supposed to do? It was one thing to weave her friends, who she knew so well. What could she bring here of herself?

With no warning, her own private nightmare flowered in her brain, fed by the magic. Her parents lay together on a bed. Their skins were riddled with dried smallpox sores; they stank of dead meat.

Dragging her mind from that memory, the girl stumbled into another, a windowless room filled with black velvet shadows. In its center was a silk braid that flickered with light: her first magic. She had worked it because she would try anything to keep back the dark, even call on magic she was certain she did not have.

Except that she'd had it. The braid glowed, as long as her mind was locked on it. It had glowed, and she survived captivity in that hidden room until Niko had found her. "I was looking for treasure," he'd said once, except the treasure was hers: a new life, and magic, and friends who were more than life.

Now she was at the end of her own stripe, having fed her shuttle through without knowing it. Time to close herself off. Carefully, she added a white cotton border, then picked the shuttle with Daja's thread. That was simple weaving, after all their dealings with Polyam. Daja was the sea. She was the fire in the forge, and a plain-capped staff. She was Sandry's first friend at Winding Circle; she was hot metal and crimson, the Trader color for mourning.

Sandry gave Daja, and the edge of the cloth, a white border.

Her back cramped. She needed to stretch. As she stood with a groan, her sensitive nose caught the enticing smell of food. Someone had left a tray on the table with a pitcher of juice, a plate of couscous and chicken, a cup of spicy chickpeas, and a platter of unleavened bread. Using her fingers she scooped up couscous as the people of Bijan and Sotat did and jammed it into her mouth. She reached for the pitcher with her free hand, meaning to pour a goblet full of juice.

"Allow me," a velvet-soft voice said as a hand lifted the pitcher. Sandry yelped, and jumped, and choked. Her uncle pounded her firmly on the back until she caught her breath, then offered her a cup of juice. She drank slowly, beet-red with embarrassment that he had seen her eating like a commoner.

"I didn't mean to startle you," Duke Vedris remarked, taking a seat. "It never occurred to me that you were not aware that I was here."

Sandry cleared her throat. "For how long?"

"For some time," he admitted. "I didn't want to interrupt. It was fascinating to watch—did you know that you were glowing?"

Sandry shook her head, still blushing.

"Eat." He nodded at the food. "You look ravenous."

"I am," she admitted, taking a chair. Picking up

her napkin, she wiped her greasy hand thoroughly. "Shouldn't you be at supper?"

"It was over an hour ago." His deep-set brown eyes glittered with amusement. "Your friends went for a walk, rather than interrupt you. Did I hear Dedicate Lark correctly? They have no magic until you are done?" He put food onto a plate for her, his big swordsman's hands graceful as he handled the utensils.

"None," she admitted, picking up her fork with properly bred daintiness. "So I'm trying to do as much tonight as I can." She began to eat, quickly but neatly.

The duke said nothing more for a while, but poured juice for himself. When she had devoured nearly half of what he'd set before her, Sandry took a breath and sat back. Her uncle was gazing through the doors that opened onto the balcony. The smoke that came in on the night breeze didn't seem to bother him.

There was something she wanted to ask. "Would you have been able to do much for Gold Ridge? Or would it have been bad, if we hadn't found the copper?"

He didn't turn his head, but his eyes shifted in her direction.

"It's good we found the copper," Sandry answered herself. Many people said they found her great-uncle impossible to fathom, but she rarely had trouble guessing his thoughts.

"My treasury is perilously low," he admitted. With a sigh, he turned to face her. "Damages from the earthquake and pirate attacks drained off my surplus cash, and the funds I have must be spread through not just Gold Ridge, but all of the northlands. With copper being mined here once again, it can be traded for supplies—*if* they can get enough from the ground. There is little time before winter closes these mountains in."

Peering in a covered dish, Sandry discovered a pudding and began to eat it with a good will. "I'm glad we've been able to help, Uncle."

The duke gently tugged one of her braids. "I am glad, too. You and your friends saved me from unpleasant choices, at least for Inoulia's lands."

Once the supper dishes were cleared, a few people brought musical instruments to the main hall and began to play. After the duke returned, Niko created illusions to amuse those who had stayed. Lark juggled a collection of plates and tableware to much applause, and two household guards performed a sword dance. Other talented people came forward, with the result that it was very late when Daja, Tris, Briar, and their teachers went to their rooms. Sandry was curled up in a chair, asleep. Her loom lay flat on the floor, with four inches of clean stripes after the section where fibers had created a satinlike cloth. The green, white, blue and orange-red stripes were not purely colored: the fibers still mingled enough to give lights in all four shades to each stripe. The white cotton barriers between the stripes were solid, though, and the cloth was ready to be cut from the loom.

Daja knelt and pressed a hand to the stripe that glowed like the heart of a fire. She felt the heat of embers on her palm, a warmth that grew up her arm to sprout limbs and branches within her flesh. Her veins filled with fire. Her magic blazed inside her once more.

Briar set a palm to the green stripe, Tris to the white. Pale fire rolled and twined through their bodies, blazing out through their eyes before it began to shrink—not to vanish, but to settle into their very bones. Daja looked at Sandry and realized that her friend had already reclaimed her own power.

"So now, with luck and hope, you will be settled," Rosethorn announced with satisfaction.

"They won't have just one kind of magic," Niko reminded her. "Briar's power is still bound to fire and lightning. You'll have to work with him, to discover what he can do."

"Could we work with me later, instead of now?" Briar yawned hugely. "It's past my bedtime."

Tris stumbled into her room without a word to anyone. Daja waved to Frostpine—who waved back—and followed the redhead.

"Go to bed, urchin," Rosethorn told Briar, her eyes amused. "We'll have all winter to explore your power."

Frostpine picked up Sandry, who fussed a little. "Back to sleep, weaver," he said quietly. "You did a giant's work today."

10

Just after breakfast the next day, Daja thought it would be a good idea to give her iron vine one last, complete going-over before the Traders came for it. Tiptoeing in and out of the girls' bedroom—Sandry was not yet awake—she got her creation and took it into the main room. Propping it on a wooden chair, she went over it by hand and by eye, fingering each stem, leaf and blossom. It had eaten all of Polyam's copper plate, translating metal into flower buds. Many of them had opened roselike blooms like the one she'd planted in the glacier valley; a few were still half-open or tightly closed. There were as many leaves as flowers; tiny iron buds on all of the branches hinted at more leaves to come.

Her exploration told her that the vine had reached the limits of its growth. It needed more iron for the remaining leaves to open, and the large stems were a bit fragile. There was something else not right with it, though she had no idea what it was.

Still, the metal felt good in her hands. Closing her eyes to concentrate on the power that trickled through the vine, she realized that while this was not the kind of magic that she had learned as Frostpine's student, it felt every bit as familiar. Could she do this again? she wondered, with growing interest. Could she create more living metal?

She thought that maybe she could.

Briar had watched as she inspected the vine. When she looked up, he commented, "It needs repotting. Actually, it needs *a* pot. And there's something not right with it."

She had never thought to get advice on care from him or from Rosethorn. "You think so?" she asked.

"I *know* so." He jerked his head toward the vine and raised his eyebrows. Daja nodded, understanding, and moved back so he could handle her creation. Briar went over it as she had, by sight and by feel. When he got to the trunk, he lifted the whole vine. "*I* know what's wrong. It's got no roots."

"Does it need them?" she asked.

"Well, the flower you poked in the ground yesterday sure put them down in a hurry." Rosethorn and Tris had come in. Briar asked the woman, "Doesn't this thing need roots?"

"If you want it to live it does. A pot wouldn't hurt, either." Rosethorn drew some copper coins out of her belt-purse. "Buy a clay pot the size of a bushel basket. This will cover the cost, if the potter isn't a robber."

"I can pay you back when I get the money from Polyam," Daja offered. It was nice to know she now could repay Rosethorn and Lark for the things they'd bought her in the past.

Rosethorn waved the offer away. "It's my contribution to this"—she looked at the vine, fumbling for a word—"experiment. Have you some iron to put in the pot with it?"

"I have scraps from the nails I've made." Daja went to get them.

When she returned, Tris was looking at the vine over Briar's shoulder. "I don't think I realized it before," she said, her voice hoarse, "but from overhead it looks like a cyclone." She pointed to the cleft where the branches split away from the vine's main stem. "See? The rods in the trunk all twist in the same direction, to make a funnel. Or you *could* say it looks like water going down a drain." She started to cough from the smoky air. Rosethorn gave her a cup of juice, frowning.

While Daja got her scraps, Lark had joined the group in the main room. Now the dedicate looked down at the vine from overhead. "To me it looks like yarn," she said, interested. "After several threads are spun together into one thick one. And the trunk is the single thick length."

"It still needs a root," Briar said. "C'mon, Daj'. Let's find that potter."

"You think those scraps will keep it fed?" she asked, trotting after him.

"Should do, unless the Traders don't mean to sell it for a while." In the hall outside he slowed to a walk as she caught up. "Just tell Polyam to give it more iron. Did you feel the power in it? It wants to grow more, but I don't think it wants to grow a lot. What do *you* get off it?"

Daja thought about that. "It's young," she remarked slowly. "Right now it's still full of fire, and the copper helps feed that. Its iron nature should take over in a month or two, though. Iron isn't a leaping kind of metal. It's just lively now with all that magic in it."

They clattered down the steps and out the door. "Cold'll make it hunker down, too," Briar said.

"Remind me to tell them to watch the stems and twigs in the cold," said Daja. The main courtyard was packed with refugees. The two mages ducked and dodged around people and wagons as they crossed it. "They'll go brittle and break off if the people handling it aren't careful."

The potter sold them not only a round green pot

of the right size, but he let them have some of his discarded clay. They got enough of that to fill their pot almost to the brim. Daja spent the next hour under Rosethorn's direction, placing gravel at the bottom of the pot for drainage, then a layer of clay, a layer of scraps, a fresh layer of clay, and so on, until the vine was firmly planted and its weight supported by its new foundation.

"If you hadn't closed the deal, I'd say charge the *Tsaw'ha* for the pot and clay," Briar remarked when they were done. "You don't want them thinking you'll give them free things all the time."

"I think Polyam at least understands I won't do that," Daja said drily. "And it sounds like she'll be doing business with us again."

"A pity that, whenever you do, she'll have to get painted up and *qunsuanen* and all," Tris said raspily. Rosethorn had finally ordered her to wear one of Sandry's finest gauze scarves over her mouth and nose.

"Who would have thought that you'd learn so much Tradertalk on this journey?" Lark teased.

They could see Tris's grin under the scarf.

"Daja, are you free?" Niko asked from the doorway. "If you are, Tris and I need you to show us the route you followed underground—" He began to cough. Once he caught his breath, he continued in a whisper. "We need to find the hot springs near the glacier. And where's Sandry?"

"Abed still," replied Lark. "She's all right—just tired."

Rosethorn had gone to her room the moment Niko started to cough. Now she returned with her syrup and a firm look in her eye. "I *thought* you were having trouble last night. Drink this." She poured some into a cup and held it out to him.

Niko looked at it as if she offered him rotten fish. "I am fine. I am per—" He couldn't even finish the sentence for coughing.

"It's not bad," said Tris, crossing her fingers behind her back. "Really. Tastes like—like mangoes."

Niko looked at her, then took the cup and downed its contents. The four watched with interest as his cheeks turned pale, then scarlet. "That's *terrible!*" he cried, his voice a thin squeak.

"Maybe I was thinking of some other syrup," Tris remarked with a straight face.

Daja found another of Sandry's finely woven lengths of gauze. "She'll run out of scarves at this rate," remarked Daja cheerfully, handing the cloth to Niko. He tied it over his nose and mouth.

Rosethorn looked at Lark. "I know the people who live here must exist with air like this, but we don't," she pointed out. "I want to ask the duke when he plans to move on."

"He's with Lady Inoulia in her library," said Niko, clearing his throat. As Rosethorn left them, he said, "Now, Daja, if you will?"

"But I don't want to enter the lava," she protested. "It would have killed me last time if the fire-grid I made hadn't come down there to protect me."

"I'll handle the lava." Frostpine came in, rubbing a towel through his damp mane. "We finished the caravan's forge-work," he explained. "Now I can put my other talents to use."

"Won't the lava melt you too?" Daja asked.

"It can *try*," he said with a grin, sitting cross-legged on the floor. He waved her down beside him. The moment his hard fingers wrapped around hers, Daja felt better. He wouldn't let any harm come to her.

Niko and Tris joined them. They were just about to start when Briar ordered them to create a space for him. He had been with Daja too, he pointed out; perhaps his experience would be of use. As they settled, Lark took Little Bear for a walk, to keep him from wading into their circle and licking their faces, as was his habit.

All five joined hands, closed their eyes, and breathed in, counting to seven. They stopped; held their breaths for another count of seven, then released as slowly as they had inhaled. Briar, Daja, and Tris were instantly together in their magic: Tris wondered if they could ever be truly apart. Soon they felt the approach of Niko and Frostpine, the fire of the men's power blazing not just hotter, but smaller, than their own, as if they filled less space with more intensity.

Daja, Briar? Lead the way, Niko said.

At first Daja wasn't sure of her path, until she remembered all she had to do was drop. The hot springs filled a vast bubble in the ground under Gold Ridge castle. Down she sped through stones, bits of metal, air, more stone, and mineral-soaked ground, until she popped into a huge rock chamber. *I started here*, she said, looking around. *And I left through one of the springs. . . .*

That one, Briar told them, directing their attention to it. *I saw her go into that one.*

Daja led as they raced through water heated far beyond what their bodies could stand. When she felt rising heat, she slowed. There was no grid to save her from the lava this time, nothing to prevent her being melted down. With the instinct of every nail, wire, blade, or strap she had ever forged, she dreaded that immense heat as it loomed nearer.

Tris raced by her.

Don't! cried Daja. *That way's the lava! You'll get—*

The hot mass rose before them, its volcanic heat beating on their power. Daja shrank back. Tris, still moving, struck it and sank like a hot iron in snow. The others felt bliss drift back from the place where she had entered the molten rock.

Her nature cannot be harmed by it, Niko explained, halting beside Daja. *Her magic helps her to mingle with it.*

Daja was vexed with herself, resentful of her friend. How could she forget that Tris was at home deep inside the earth? It wasn't fair! *She* was the smith-mage, not Tris Chandler—why couldn't *she* exist here?

I don't know about Tris, but my roots are starting to crisp, Briar complained. *How can we pass this stuff?*

My power has no connection to it—I can pass easily, said Niko. *Frostpine?*

Out of the miniature sun that was the other man drifted a large, shieldlike plate of white fire. *Briar, Daja, get behind this,* Frostpine ordered. *Daja, remind me, when things are quiet, to teach you how to do this for yourself.*

Briar and Daja tucked themselves behind Frostpine's creation. The moment the shield stood between them and the lava, the awful pressure of that immense heat fell off. They felt its power grow as they advanced, but it was no longer impossible to bear.

Dripping from the vein in the ground, they entered the molten rock. Bubblelike, Frostpine's shield spread and encircled them. *Which way, Daja?* the smith-mage asked.

She pointed to an opening overhead, different from the entrance they had used.

Tris, come on! called Niko, drifting freely beside their shield. *We have work to do!*

They sped toward Daja's escape route and passed through. Frostpine's shield evaporated. Now that the dreadful heat was behind them, Daja happily took the lead, speeding through the many cracks in earth and stone. Open air beckoned, and she leaped into it gladly. She was aboveground, and safe.

Frostpine, Briar, Niko, and lastly Tris soared out of the pools of the mountain hot springs, their magical forms pale light-globes to Daja's vision. The water and boiling mud showed not even a ripple to mark their passage. She watched, fascinated. They were all so strong in this form, but in terms of the physical world, they didn't really exist.

The glacier valley is through those trees, she told them. *Now what?*

Now we see if the faults—the cracks in the stone— reach from here to some place well under the glacier, said Niko. *Will you help us, you and Frostpine?*

She wanted to stay here, in open air. The thought of getting so near to the lava again gave her the shudders.

I can do it, said Frostpine.

Can I help? Briar wanted to know. *The tree-roots here run into some of those cracks you want.*

That shamed Daja—everyone wanted to work but her. Taking her courage in hand, she followed them back into the ground.

Tris brought up the rear, keeping an eye on the cracks that fed the hot springs and, much farther below, the lava that heated them. How close to the underside of the glacier might the warmth—from molten rock or from boiling water—come?

They soon found a series of cuts in the ground that paralleled the mountains on the eastern side of the glacier. Several came to dead ends. At last they found a deep fault between two gigantic slabs of granite that crossed miles beneath the ice river. It reached back under the mountain hot springs. Niko spread himself through the ground in every direction, then rose up into the glacier ice to see how deep it was.

We must be very careful. So careful that I'm not sure it can be done, he told them at last. *If we bring the lava too close to the surface, there's a chance it can blow through the glacier.*

Niko! cried Tris. *It's almost five hundred feet thick up there! And I wouldn't use a lot of lava!*

There are crevasses in that ice, said Niko. *Once your lava breaks through into open air, do you really believe you can stop the force in a volcano?*

There was nothing Tris could say to that. She had tried to counteract the power of the tides once. After reading about the fate of others who had tried similar experiments, she knew she had gotten off lightly with just a few days in bed.

We must think about this, Niko added. *As I mentioned yesterday, we have more than a volcano to worry about. There is the chance of floods and mud slides.*

Why did we bother coming, then, if you don't believe it can be done? Briar demanded. He wanted to find Rosethorn and tell her that tiny plants grew in the ice. He *didn't* want to sit here listening to Niko fuss.

Because it can *be done*, was the stern reply. *Are we to have another chat about rushing in with magic?*

No, Niko, chorused Briar, Tris, and Daja.

Then start exploring. All five of us should know the ice and ground in this area by heart.

When they returned to their bodies, it was almost noon. Polyam, Rosethorn, and Lark were on the balcony with Little Bear and Shriek, talking as they fed the bird egg balls. Hearing groans as the five explorers tried to make stiff bodies work again, the women came to help them rise. Sandry, just waking up, rushed in to lend a hand.

Once everyone was comfortable, Polyam retrieved a wooden box she had placed on a small table. "Our caravan is leaving this afternoon, now that Master Firetamer assures us the grassfires near the south road are out," she announced formally. "It is time to conclude our bargain."

The box was a beautiful thing, glossy carved wood inlaid with mother-of-pearl. When Polyam opened it, they saw that it was lined with soft black velvet.

Gently Daja set the potted iron vine on the big table. Polyam opened a washed-leather bag that lay in the box and drew out five gold coins. Two were three inches across, the size of medallions rather than money. On one side was the coat of arms of the ruling dukes of Emelan: a ship with a lighthouse on either side, the rune for protection on top, and an enclosed spiral below. On the other side was the image of a harbor, its opening guarded on the left by a massive, rectangular tower and on the right by a thin spiky tower perched on a lump of rock. It was an exact portrait of Summersea harbor.

"Strike me sideways," muttered Briar. His fingers itched to handle the coins. How many people got to see a gold maja in a lifetime? Until this sight of money, the long round of bargaining had been a game. Now it wasn't.

With the slow care of ceremony, Polyam set each maja down before the plant. Beside them she placed three smaller coins, gold astrels.

"I am satisfied," Daja said automatically, though she wasn't. The money had never really interested her, only the chance to talk with a Trader again. Now that chance was ending. When Polyam—and her caravan—left, Daja would be alone among the *kaqs* once more.

Briar gathered up the coins and offered them to Daja. She turned her head away. After a brief hesitation, the boy passed them to Lark, who tucked them into her belt-purse.

When Polyam looked at the vine and sighed, Daja said quickly, "I'll help you take it back. There's a wheelbarrow we can use. And I'd like to go with the caravan a ways—well, behind it, with Polyam," she said, looking to Frostpine and Niko for permission. "I'll come back by dark." When they hesitated, she added, "If it's safe enough for them to leave, it's safe enough for me to walk, surely."

"There you all are." Lady Inoulia stood in the open door. "Are you hungry? I wish to invite Lady Sandrilene, and you mages—and your little pupils, of course—to midday on our lookout tower. Yarrun has something to show us. My lord duke has already accepted." Glancing at Polyam, she added, "I know you are anxious to be on your way, *wirok*."

Daja looked down, clenching her teeth at the barely hidden dismissal in the lady's words. "I must refuse," she said coldly. "I am helping Polyam of Tenth Caravan Idaram take her goods to her people." *And I hope they cheat you, and your children, and your grandchildren, in every trade they do with you forevermore*, she added silently. *Kaq*.

The other three young people looked uncomfortable, but unlike Daja, they had no excuse ready. Niko accepted for them all and agreed to come to the tower when the noon bell struck.

"You should keep this," Polyam said, pushing the inlaid box away from her. "The caravan would only burn it, and that would be a waste of good work. Besides, there's a brick of Trader tea under the velvet—I had to smuggle it out."

"Thank you," whispered Daja.

"And I thank *you*," said Polyam. She bowed to Lark, Rosethorn, Niko, and Frostpine. "It was an honor to meet all of you. I've heard your names for years.

What a pleasure it is to find that you deserve all the praise that has been given to you, and more."

They bowed to her in return. "May your road be easy and your profits great," Lark said in Tradertalk.

Polyam shrugged. "I doubt that," she said wryly, re-settling her grip on her staff. "I go back to being just the *wirok* now—after ten days of trailing the caravan and washing in every pond and stream. It was nice, being almost as good as a *daka*." She looked at Daja's friends. "We will meet again. The *gilav* intends to make Winding Circle a stop on our route."

Once Daja loaded the plant into the barrow lent them by the potter, Polyam bowed awkwardly in farewell and led the way out of the room.

Lark sighed. "If we're to join her ladyship and her pet mage, let's neaten up."

When Daja and Polyam emerged from the band of forest just below the castle into the clearing around the main road, the girl could see that Tenth Caravan Idaram was ready to go. Everyone was packed and loaded. Families were eating a cold midday meal, older children keeping a strict watch on goats, horses, or the occasional cow. Mothers served food and ate with their babies already in slings on their backs. Men and boys checked their weapons. Even the dogs knew to stay close.

Daja halted just under the trees, fighting to swallow the lump that had appeared in her throat. The means of travel was so different, but some things were the same: White or Blue Traders, they fixed vivid blue pompoms and strings of bells to their gear to scare away demons. The babies wore blue strings on their wrists, and every child under the age of two wore tiny golden bell earrings. Many girls wore an ankle bracelet of tiny bells, the boys azure blue wrist bands. The men and most of the children wore leggings and thigh-length tunics; women and older girls wore flaring skirts, short-sleeved blouses, and long vests. Until her family's ship sank, Daja had spent her entire life among people who had dressed and decorated things in just this way.

"Over here," Polyam said, going to a small, rickety cart. It and the elderly donkey that pulled it had been placed near the trees. Daja blinked at it, dazzled. The wood had been painted bright yellow; yellow pompoms fluttered from the donkey's harness.

"I get to cleanse the donkey, too," Polyam muttered as she helped Daja lift the plant into the back of the cart. "In every pond and stream."

Daja got into the cart—something Polyam would have trouble doing—to strap the pot down. She fastened the ties that would keep it from bouncing with quick, efficient seamen's knots. As she worked, she kept her head down so she wouldn't see the Traders murmuring to each other and looking away from her.

"Are you sorry this happened?" she asked Polyam, keeping her voice low.

The *wirok* leaned against the side of the cart. "I don't believe I am, *qunsuanen* and all," she replied, also quiet. "It's made me appreciate being *Tsaw'ha* still, I can tell you that." She looked at her kinfolk. One corner of her broad mouth twisted down, making her face suddenly harsh. "Have you nothing better to gawk at?" she demanded loudly. "Haven't you seen a *trangshi* before?"

Daja peeked at the other Traders. They had suddenly found things to do that gave them an excuse to turn away. She grinned suddenly. It was hard—almost impossible—to feel sorry for the *wirok*, just now, and much easier to feel sorry for the rest of Tenth Caravan Idaram.

"I'll never see any of this in the same way, either," Polyam admitted, her voice soft again. "I used to think they were right, and I was wrong."

Daja gaped at her. "That's what *I* used to think."

"And now you wonder if you aren't more right, and our people more wrong?" asked Polyam.

Daja hesitated, then nodded.

"So we both learned something," Polyam told her. "And who knows? Maybe it was something we needed to learn."

A lean, craggy-faced man who wore the short green-and-orange-striped cape of the journey leader raised his staff and gave a high, long, trilling cry. Women throughout the caravan added their own trills to his until Daja thought the trees would shake from

185

the sound. Urging his horse forward, the man set off on the road south. A handful of other riders followed. After them came the first wagon, the *gilav's*, roofed with canvas painted in eye-smarting colors and trimmed in brightly polished brass. Other wagons, mounted riders, and people on foot began to move as the caravan got underway.

Polyam clambered awkwardly onto the seat of the cart, cursing as her wooden leg got jammed. At least Daja knew better than to offer help. Once Polyam had freed herself and settled, Daja climbed up beside her and slid her own staff into the back of the cart with Polyam's. For a brief, brief moment, at least, Daja Kisubo was a Trader again.

11

The meal laid for them on the high tower that Daja had climbed the day before was an excellent one, with two kinds of soup, venison, cold chicken, and fresh-baked rolls. Lady Inoulia waited until everyone had been served wine or fruit juice before she spoke. When all her lunch guests held full goblets, she rested a regal hand on Yarrun's green-brocaded shoulder. Yarrun himself was smiling. Briar looked him over and frowned. The mage was trembling from top to toe. Daja had mentioned that Yarrun was taking stimulants; had he used too many?

"Your grace," the lady said to Duke Vedris, who nodded, "Master Niklaren, guests. As of this morning, each and every wildfire in this entire valley is—extinguished."

Does she want us to applaud? Sandry asked her friends through their magical bond.

"Extinguished?" asked Rosethorn, fine brows drawn together in a tiny frown. "All of them?" She went to the battlement. "Are you sure?"

"I would hardly claim they were, if they were not," Yarrun replied waspishly. "You wasted your students' time in preparing burn medicines, as I told you. The grassfires have used up their fuel, and the forests are untouched."

"I think that my mage does beautiful work," said Lady Inoulia. "I had hoped you could be more generous to him."

"What if fire got into the bottom-most layer of mast, deep under the trees?" demanded Rosethorn. "It could smolder for days, unseen, building in power."

"I tell you it has *not*," Yarrun snapped. "Why can you not admit that academic magic does things nature magic cannot?"

Lark went to the rail. "It's an impressive feat," she said, her gaze on the valley. "Rosie isn't trying to take that from you—"

"Is she not!" cried the Gold Ridge mage.

"If you would just calm down," Niko said, his thick brows knitted in a frown like Rosethorn's. His concern, though, seemed to be for the other man. "Take a seat—"

Yarrun was sweating and pale. He stared at Niko with bloodshot eyes. "I am not one of your child-wizards, in need of coddling," he hissed.

The duke took a seat, his eyes on the mages. Inoulia draped herself in a chair close to his. "They have uses," Sandry heard her murmur to the duke, "but when these people get to one of their endless debates—!"

Tris wanted no part of the fight that was developing. Walking to the eastern edge of the platform, she stared at the view. There lay the village and southern road; past them she saw heavy forest and steeply rising mountains. Behind her she could hear Niko talking softly to Yarrun, and Lark to Rosethorn.

One eye on his teacher, Briar eased over to the table. Under the disapproving gaze of the servants he picked through a dish of berries. Sandry joined him, though she left the fruit alone.

"I can't wait till we leave," she murmured to him. "I've had enough of these people."

Briar grinned and rested a berry on her lower lip. "Open wide," he ordered.

Uh-oh, said a magical voice.

They turned to stare at Tris.

Uh-oh, she repeated. She didn't seem to know that Briar and Sandry could hear. *Uh-oh, uh-oh . . .*

Stop it, Briar ordered in mind-talk as he and Sandry went to her. *It's idiotic and you'll make us*—crazy, he was about to add, but the sight below chased all

189

thought from his mind. Billows of smoke rose in the eastern forest. They took shape not on the far rim or the southern edge, near charred grasslands and the firebreak, but at a spot a mile inside the woods.

"Someone's burning leaves," Sandry remarked flatly.

Flame raced up a lone, dead tree. Smoke eddied through the forest around it.

"Rosethorn," squeaked Briar. He cleared his throat. "Rosethorn," he repeated, louder this time. "Niko."

Something in his voice brought Rosethorn at a run. "Sweet Mila of the grain. *Yarrun!*" she cried.

Everyone came over. Lady Inoulia gasped as the patch of smoke thickened, rising in a circle around the flaming tree. "Do something!" she ordered Yarrun.

He gave her a scornful look and fumbled in his belt-pouch. Producing a small, round bottle, he placed it on the stone rail. "Where did it come from?" he muttered to himself.

Niko stepped up beside him and briefly shut his eyes. The three young people shielded their own eyes as his power blazed out. Squinting, they saw that Niko had opened his eyes and was holding out his hands, palm up. A window opened in the air. Through it they saw, not pines and leafy trees, but limbs and trunks without greenery, and ground covered with masses of sticks and a glassy blanket. When they looked to the spot where the smoke had appeared, they could see that a dull orange glow lay under the glass blanket, spreading there like a stain in water.

The window vanished; Niko ceased to glow. "Rosethorn was right," he said flatly. "Somehow fire got into the piled-up mast on the forest floor. I'm no specialist, but I would say this blaze has been growing for most of the day."

"Impossible!" Yarrun brushed his hair back with a quivering hand. "I would have sensed it!"

Niko met his eyes. "Would you?" he asked evenly. "Even my students can tell you are exhausted."

Yarrun bit his lip. "You want to see me fail."

Niko continued to gaze at him, black eyes level, even kind. It was Yarrun who looked away.

Sandry grabbed Tris's shoulder. Flames now appeared in the crowns of those trees circling the dead one. The smoke that rose from the ground there spread as the undergrowth caught fire. Impatiently Tris shook off Sandry's grip and stretched a hand out to Yarrun. "Can you use my strength?" she asked. "I don't know the spells, but—"

"I know them," said Niko. "Good idea, Tris. Yarrun, you may have mine as well—"

"Gods rot you both!" shrieked Yarrun, his face dripping sweat. "I don't need help!"

Hurt, Tris backed away.

Yarrun dumped a pile of glittering dust from his vial onto the stone rail. With a hand that shook he drew a circle in it, his lips moving. The dust began to rise, not as the breeze tugged it, but against the air's motion. It hovered, then settled back onto the rail.

"I can do this," Yarrun growled. It wasn't clear whom he spoke to, and none of them replied. He scraped the dust into a small pile with the edges of his hands.

Stepping back, Niko used Briar for concealment as he reached behind the boy to pluck Tris's sleeve. She looked at him with a puzzled frown while Briar, deadpan, gazed straight ahead. Niko pursed his lips and blew. Tris guessed that he wanted her to help Yarrun's dust to reach the fire and nodded.

Yarrun nicked a vein in his left wrist with his belt-knife and let a few drops of blood fall onto the dust. Frostpine started to protest and stopped at Niko's sharp gesture. The only sounds were the hiss of the wind and Yarrun's hoarse, open-mouthed breathing. He swayed; when Duke Vedris moved to brace him, he shook the duke off.

Tris stepped back into the shadows beside the kiosk. Reaching into the breeze, she grabbed a fistful of moving air.

Again Yarrun drew a circle in the dust. This time the wet powder followed his finger in a trickle, as if he'd added more than a few drops of blood. He raised his hands, lips moving. The dust flowed into the open air, spreading until it formed a thin scarf.

Tris flung out her handful of trapped wind. It

rushed from her grip, strengthened by its captivity, and pulled the scarf of dust away from the tower in its wake. Lady Inoulia and the duke felt the air's passage and turned to stare at Tris. The redhead was leaning against the kiosk, her face to its stone wall, as if she were too afraid to watch Yarrun—as if she were too upset to have done anything. The lady turned her attention back to her mage. When Tris straightened and looked up, the duke still had his eye on her. Slowly he winked. Then he moved to the rail to watch the sparkling powder as it raced toward the smoke.

Now Yarrun was chanting, hoarse-voiced. His bony fingers cut the air, leaving trails of light for the mages to see. His voice climbed in volume; everyone stepped back from him as the power in his signs flew after the dust. Louder and louder he spoke, until the last three words were a scream. He dropped his hands, swaying.

Far below, the fire in the dead tree went out.

"Aha!" he bellowed. "And again I have done it! While—"

Mutely the duke nodded to a spot west of the original blaze, on the edge of the thin groove of the road. Smoke rose there. Yarrun pointed to it and shrieked something; the smoke blew apart. Nearby an oak, its leaves turning color, showed darts of flame. Yarrun pointed and spoke again; the fire vanished.

New smoke rose in four places close to the original blaze at the dead tree. Yarrun dealt with two. When he addressed the third, his voice was nearly gone. He staggered, pointed, opened his mouth to speak—and collapsed. Frostpine caught him and lowered him gently, turning his body so his face was visible.

Blood ran from one nostril, slowed, and stopped. Yarrun's eyes were open; the veins in his left eye had burst, turning the white a dull crimson. He was dead.

Rosethorn knelt beside him and closed his eyes with her fingers.

"We're in trouble now," whispered Briar.

Lady Inoulia leaned over the battlement to stare down at the forest. The dead tree was burning again; so were many green trees around it. Half a mile from the east side of the road smoke rolled through the leafy canopy. It formed a mile-long dark band from the spot where they'd first seen it to a point near the castle. "Can you put it out?" she demanded, without turning away from the view. "I know this isn't your kind of work, Master Goldeye, but—so many mages—can't one of you stop it?"

"One of us tried," Rosethorn said flatly. She still knelt beside Yarrun. "You saw the result. I warned him what happens when these things get started. I'll tell you now—it's too late to put the fire out."

Inoulia, confused, turned to look at Rosethorn. "What do you mean? It's never too late to stop a fire—"

"This fire has burned for hours," Frostpine said

quietly. "The longer it goes, the more force it gathers. Nature is slow to begin, but once she does, her works have their own hard power. *Any* mage who tries to command that fire like Yarrun did will die."

Inoulia clenched her hands. "The village," she said abruptly. "They'll be trapped." Raising her skirts, she raced down the stairs, her servants following.

Niko and Lark traded quick looks. "Stay here," Niko ordered the three young people. When they nodded, he and Lark followed Inoulia into the castle.

"Yarrun *died* for her," Sandry remarked bitterly. "Doesn't she *care?*"

"Grief must wait until her people are safe," the duke told her. "That comes first."

"Then grief may have a long wait," Rosethorn said. She hugged herself, her face gray. "The fire's going into the crowns of the trees."

Frostpine, who still held Yarrun, glared at her. "What does *that* mean?"

"It'll speed up," Rosethorn wearily explained.

"I had best see what I may do for Inoulia," said the duke. He kissed Sandry, and left them.

Briar, Tris, and Sandry rushed to the battlement. The treetops were ablaze. As they watched, the fire jumped the road in three places, catching hold on the other side.

"Daja's there!" cried Sandry, horrified. "Daja, and the caravan!"

*   *   *

At first Daja had ignored the thickening smoke. She was too busy watching the wagons and listening to the rise and fall of Trader voices from the road ahead.

"I'll be glad to see the last of this place," remarked Polyam after a burst of coughing. "The grassfires weren't so bad, the last time we came here. Old Yarrun is losing his touch."

"Not to hear him tell it," replied Daja.

Polyam snorted. "Four years ago, six, he wouldn't have let even grasslands burn. He took it as a matter of pride that he could stop any blaze in the valley. Once he accused the cook of giving him the nobles' *leftovers* for his midday? He stopped all the fires in the kitchen. Nowhere else—just the kitchen. *That's* how much control he had." She looked sidelong at Daja. "I hope you and your friends don't go all prideful like that. So many do—mages, that is."

"We make too many mistakes to get prideful," Daja assured her. Something was bothering her. The exposed skin on her left felt tight and stretched, as if—

As if I was at the forge and working close to the fire, she realized. As if I was really, really *hot*.

Balancing herself one-handed on Polyam's shoulder, ignoring the woman's protest, she stood on the driver's bench and turned her nose into the wind. It came out of the east, to her left, along with the worst of the smoke and that feeling of too much heat. She sent her magic out in a widening arc, like ripples on a pond.

The knowledge of fire roaring out of control smote her chest, making her stagger.

"This is no time for trick riding!" snapped Polyam. "What are you up to?"

Daja sat. "How much farther till we're clear of the woods?" she demanded. "I don't remember how long this part of the road is. Polyam, quick!"

"Another three miles, give or take. Why?" Polyam coughed as thick coils of smoke rolled across the sunken road.

We'll never make it, Daja realized. "We have to go back. There's still time."

"Go back? Whatever for?" Polyam was barely able to speak for coughing.

Daja! cried Sandry's voice in her mind. *Make them turn around! The forest is burning!*

Daja cupped her hands around her mouth. "Stop!" she yelled at the top of her lungs. "Halt!"

A boy looked back, as did two drivers. When they saw who spoke to them, they turned away.

"Polyam, *tell* them!" cried Daja, yanking on the woman's shoulder.

"Tell them?" Polyam demanded. "Tell them what?"

"The forest is burning!" cried Daja. "We're riding into it!" When Polyam hesitated, Daja snapped, "I'm in contact with Sandry—she can see it from the castle!"

Polyam looked at the trees and the smoke. She thrust the reins at Daja and yanked her staff from the back of the cart. "Wait," she ordered. "And hold 'em." Slipping from the bench, she landed on the ground and staggered, her wooden leg sliding. With the skill of practice, she stopped her fall and lurched into motion on the road, using her staff to pull her along.

"Where's the *mimander?*" she yelled. "Everybody halt! I need the *mimander,* I need the *gilav*—" She stopped to cough helplessly. The moment she got herself under control she moved forward, shouting for the leaders of the caravan.

Daja ground her teeth. Everyone ignored the yellow-decked Polyam. Of course, thought Daja grimly; she's unclean because of her contact with me. They won't hear her till she's washed me from her skin.

Rising to her feet, Daja filled her lungs. Her ribs served as a bellows—smoke had no effect on a bellows—as she cried in a booming voice, "Halt right now, or by Hakkoi I'll rust every nail in the caravan! I can do it!" She couldn't, but the Traders didn't know that. "Every ring, every buckle!"

The closest wagon slowed, then stopped. So did the wagon ahead of it.

So, thought Daja, grimly pleased, you just have to know how to talk to them. *Where is it?* she mind-called to her friends on the tower. *Where is the fire?* Was that a flicker of orange off to her left?

It's half a mile ahead of the caravan and it's coming at you all along the eastern edge, said Tris. *And— and—*her magical voice failed.

It jumped the road in front, Sandry told Daja somberly. *You're cut off. Make them stop, or they'll ride into it.*

Daja grabbed the reins and jumped to the ground. Dragging the donkey, she closed the gap between her and the wagon ahead and hitched the animal to it. People inside shouted, objecting to their wagon being touched by a *trangshi*; Daja ignored them. Once the donkey was securely tied, she ran to the front of the caravan, where Polyam was yelling at its leaders.

"You're cut off!" Daja cried when she was within earshot. "Turn back! The fire has jumped the road!"

"Trangshi—" snapped *gilav* Chandrisa, furious, "this has polluted us all! Was that your aim all along?"

"I don't care if you're polluted or not!" Daja cried. "I *do* care that you're riding into fire!"

"We have been too lenient," began the *gilav*.

"Enough," said a firm voice, as harsh as a crow's— Polyam's. "Mother, do as she says."

The *gilav* blinked at Polyam, who went to the heads of the ponies that drew Chandrisa's pretty wagon. Gripping the reins, Polyam began to turn the team.

The road leader urged his mount back along the string of wagons, talking to each driver. Slowly, one at a time, they started to turn around. None knew better than Traders that haste now would mean tangled harness and fouled wheels. Each worked carefully, one fearful eye on the heavy pall of smoke on the road's eastern flank.

Daja walked up to Polyam. "You never said she was your mother," commented Daja in an undertone.

"It wasn't exactly something that brought us honor, after the mountain ate my leg," was Polyam's muttered reply. Seeing Daja walk south on the road, she asked, "Where are *you* going?"

"I want to see how close we're cutting this," called Daja. The road led her up a small incline, over a rise, and across a small bridge above a dry creek. She climbed a second rise, halting at the top.

Three hundred yards before her, trees of all sizes blazed on either side of the road. The ground under them burned, reminding her of Rosethorn's words about mast. Clumps of flaming leaves—burning squirrel nests—were carried by the wind into places where there was no fire. Within seconds they had started fresh blazes.

The fire advanced, roaring as she'd once heard an earthquake roar. Daja gulped from her water bottle, thinking hard. If she allowed this fire to come on, it would overtake the Traders. They needed a chance to get wagons and animals turned in this sunken road. Somehow she would have to stop the fire's advance.

Tris? she mind-called. *This is as much your kind of thing as mine.*

She felt Tris reach out and wrap her fingers around a man's warm and bony wrist.

It is mine, too. It was Frostpine, able now to speak and hear Daja through Tris. Relief made Daja's knees weak. Frostpine would fix all this!

He looked through her eyes and whispered, *Shurri and Hakkoi.* He sounded frightened.

Daja swallowed hard. Perhaps he couldn't fix it. *What can I do?* she asked. *If I make myself into a really large bellows . . . ?*

No! Don't blow the fire back, he cautioned. *What works with candleflame won't do here. You'll just spread it.*

You have to weave it, Sandry announced, *like you did that day when Polyam gave you her plate. We'll give you the power, but you have to work it.*

Yarrun called it the Great Square of Zuhayar the Magnificent, said Tris. *It put your forge-fire out. If you make it big enough, maybe you can put this out.*

I can't make a square big enough to put out a forest fire! cried Daja.

Start weaving! urged Sandry. *Worry about putting the fire out after it's under control!*

Daja moaned, chewing on her lip. The wall of flames was advancing, with the caravan in its path. The only thing that blocked it was her.

Looking the ground over, she saw a gap in the fire where a mass of rock jutted through the soil. The road itself was another break in the wall. Perhaps what she needed was more than one fire-weaving.

Reaching out with one hand, she split her fingers

apart. The leftmost chunk of fire was her thumb, the mass directly ahead her index and middle finger, the blaze on the right her remaining fingers. She let her magic billow forward on those three paths. It swelled and bloomed, carrying power from Sandry, Tris, and Frostpine as well as Daja's own. Holding that magic with her mind, she pinched the blaze into three gigantic stems. In a way it was like handling forge-fire, except that the least quiver in her attention would free these flames to do much more damage than she could in a smithy. Pinching this fire in made it stronger, like channeling a broad river into a small, deep channel. She drew her three blazes up and sent them shooting toward the sky in pillars.

Locking her mind on the leftmost pillar, Daja ordered it to break into multiple strands on one end, like her earlier fire-weaving. This blaze fought her. It wanted to break free of her magic and go back to eating everything in sight.

"No," she growled. She had worked her will on iron and gold. This fire would do as it was bid!

The column writhed. It wanted to chew the fuel-covered ground. It did not want to submit. Daja struck hard with her magic, slamming her power down. The column wavered and split at the end like a frayed rope.

Here was Sandry, waiting in the core of Daja's magic. *I can do this,* she assured Daja. *Let me through.*

With a sigh, Daja turned her loose. Sandry raced in

to gather the ends of the frayed column of fire. As swiftly as if she'd handled fire-thread all her life, she began to weave. Daja watched briefly, worried because she could see that Sandry's grip on the many strands wasn't as firm as she would like. No matter how often the fiery threads escaped her, though, Sandry grabbed them back time after time.

Reassured, Daja looked at the fire-pillar directly before her. Now she understood better how to shape it. Using power like a hammer, she struck. The column wavered, then firmed. Daja pounded it again and again. At last the end frayed into strands. Tris took this weaving over. She wasn't as quick as Sandry, but the strands didn't escape her as they did the noble. Tris would be all right.

Daja watched her friends, clutching the last column of flame. *Thank Trader and Bookkeeper that our powers mixed,* she thought, startled. *I never could have worked this blaze all by myself.*

She fixed her mind on the column of fire she still held. This time she was confident: a single blow of her magic split it into a dozen strands.

Allow me, said Frostpine. His magic roaring through her made Daja's teeth chatter. She let him by, watching as he worked the flames not as thread but as wire. One after another he laid the strands across each other and hammered the places they crossed, melting them into a solid join.

Daja's vision grayed; her knees felt weak. All this

power running through her body was dragging at her strength. She bit her lip and forced her mind back to the job at hand.

Sandry finished her work, a long scarf of flame that towered in the air. *Remember when you lay your grid on your forge-fire?* she asked Daja now.

It went out, Daja replied, hope leaping fire-bright in her own heart.

So put out a fire with this! urged Sandry.

Certainly there were large blazes behind the three flame creations. Daja carefully drew Sandry back through her core, pulling her friend out of the fire-scarf. Once none of Sandry was left in the weaving, Daja gripped it afresh and pinched off its stem. When it was free of its trunk, she let the weaving fall to the ground.

Everything under the scarf went black, smothered. The flames close to its edges, however, blew out and away, setting a new part of the forest ablaze.

"Oh no," whispered Daja, horrified, guessing what had gone wrong. When she'd dropped her grid on the forge-fire, the edges of the stone fireplace had kept the blaze from escaping. There was nothing out here to hold the fire at the edges of the weaving in.

We'd better not try that experiment again, Sandry remarked grimly.

No indeed, Daja replied.

They watched as the last fiery threads in Frost-pine's and Tris's columns joined the rest to form tidily arranged scarves. *Done*, Tris said with relief. She trickled wearily back into Daja.

Frostpine stopped to admire his work. *Not bad for an old man like me*, he remarked. *This kind of thing has real possibilities. I'm glad I tried it.*

I'm pleased that you're pleased, Daja replied sarcastically. *If I knew you wanted to play with fire, I'd've helped you with it ages ago.*

She felt him laugh as he retreated back through her, allowing her to grip the fire-scarves alone. They blazed white with power, barring the advance of the more ordinary fires behind them. Daja scratched her head, trying to think. Now what? Ought she to try to capture the fire that had started when she and Sandry had dropped that weaving? It was taking a path away from her and the caravan. To get it, she'd have to chase it. Was she up to that?

A hand fell heavily on her shoulder and was quickly snatched away. "*Trader*, you're hot!" cried Polyam. She was coated in soot; the yellow *qunsuanen* paint was smeared. "Are you all right?"

Daja looked at her, thinking she wouldn't have suspected that anything could make Polyam look less attractive than she was already. Here was proof that something could.

Behind the woman she could see that the wagons were not moving. "What's wrong?" she demanded. "I can't hold this stuff forever, you know! Get them—"

The look on Polyam's scarred face told her their bad situation had gotten worse. "I think the fire was already headed north when you got out of the cart," the *wirok* informed her tiredly. "It jumped the road. We're cut off at the rear."

12

Rosethorn paced like a caged tigress, her eyes locked on the distant flames. "I can't stand this," she muttered. "I have to do something."

Briar was at his wits' end looking after her. Scared, he glanced across the platform: Sandry, Tris, and Frostpine stood hand in hand where they could see through drifting clouds of smoke to the shadowed groove that was the road. In Briar's vision they all glowed bright with magic.

They wouldn't be able to help. What could he do with Rosethorn? She was thinking of something foolish; he was sure of that. Just two months ago, she had thrown all of her power into a wall of thorny plants at

Winding Circle, even though pirates were dumping the burning jelly called battlefire onto them. Briar remembered Rosethorn's screams: she had felt the plants' deaths far more than did he. She meant to pitch herself into this war for green lives, he knew it.

"If you do something, let's do it *together,*" he urged. He clung to her sleeve as she made her hundredth trip around the platform. "Use me for a shield, *please*, Rosethorn!"

That made her stop. "No," she said flatly. "I'm going to save some of the trees, and I *forbid* you to help."

"No!" he yelled, grabbing fistfuls of her habit. "I won't let you!"

It felt as if he'd hugged a sapling that suddenly turned into a tree wider than the tower on which they stood. Briar was thrown back into the kiosk that sheltered the stair. The breath slammed from his lungs; he slid to the floor. The giant tree that was also Rosethorn shone so brightly he could not bear to look at her.

"My lad, do as you're told," she murmured. Then that overwhelming power—Rosethorn's, hidden until now—drew back, to his intense relief.

Someone was climbing the steps and stepping onto the platform. Cool, human hands lifted Briar to his feet and pressed a bottle to his lips. He drank. Blessedly sweet water, flavored with mint, ran down his throat, making him feel like Briar again.

"Didya see that elephant?" he asked, pushing the bottle away when he'd had enough. "I wanna complain to a magistrate. Someone let an elephant run wild, and it stepped on me."

"That was just Rosethorn being noble," said Lark grimly. "I'll make her use *my* strength—I'm not bound to green magic, so I won't get hurt. You help the girls and Frostpine. From the way he's cursing, they just ran into more trouble."

"I'll help them, too," said Niko, who had come back with her. "The fire has circled Daja and the caravan."

Briar stumbled over to Sandry and Tris, his throat tight with fear. He could see now that the line of smoke and flame had surged from the east to wrap itself around a length of the road like a giant letter C. At the top of the curve rose towering rectangles of woven fire. At the bottom of the C shadowed patches dotted the flames, each showing the silver wash of magic. Reaching with his own power, he found Rosethorn in every patch, holding off the fire with sheer strength.

Turning, he saw her nearby, half-bent over the stone rail. He moaned deep in his throat when he saw she had bitten through her bottom lip.

Lark stepped in beside Rosethorn and slung an arm around the shorter woman. "Here, love," she said kindly, "let me help you with that."

This time at least Briar knew to shade his eyes

against the blaze as Lark's magic flooded into her friend's. Jealousy rose in his throat, thick as bile. Rosethorn would take help from *Lark*.

What do you care, as long as she gets help and plenty of it? his better self wanted to know.

It still hurt.

He turned away at last, trying to blink the spots from his vision. "Well," he remarked with a sigh, "may as well make myself useful." Closing his eyes, he found the blaze that was the combined magics of Tris, Frostpine, Sandry, and Niko and plunged in. They formed a pool into which he spread himself: at its bottom, a long, silver tie flowed toward Daja like an open drain.

At first Daja thought she was trapped, unable to leave the two remaining fire-scarves. They were the only barrier against the flames in front of the caravan. If she tried to move them or take them with her, the Traders would be in danger within minutes.

I'll take them, offered Sandry. *If we rope them together, I'm nearly positive I can hold them alone.*

I'll stay too, said Frostpine. *Together we can hold them. But the rest of you had better think of a way to get rid of these things before we're exhausted.*

Be careful, Daja told Frostpine and Sandry. *Don't let them break away from you, or we'll all cook.* Reaching inside, she found her ties to the scarves and passed them to her teacher and her friend. Only when she was sure that they were in control of the fiery weavings did she head for the back of the train at a run, with Polyam following.

The Traders had formed a tight cluster at the middle of their line of wagons. The children were crying, but quietly, as Trader children were taught: they huddled under the vehicles, out of their elders' way. Except for the teams drawing the wagons, the animals were bunched at the rear, guarded by men and teenagers who kept them from escaping into the forest. Daja could smell cooking goat and chicken. Some of the animals must have run into the fire in panic. On both sides of the sunken road where she had been just half an hour ago, the forest was ablaze.

Daja's heart thumped at the sight of those walls of flame. She leaned against the last cart—the one that held her iron vine—shuddering. I can't, she thought. I *can't!* This will kill me, and for who? *Them?*

She looked at the caravan, her eyes watering. I'm *trangshi.* They keep telling me so. They'd be happier if I was dead. If they survive this, the *first* thing they'll do is put the whole caravan through *qunsuanen.*

Polyam had caught up to her. She slumped against the wood beside Daja, panting. "I wouldn't blame you if you left us to burn," she croaked, her voice thick with smoke. "We only did what our people have always done, but *Tsaw'ha* custom is cruel when you're on the wrong end of it."

Daja wiped her forehead on her sleeve. Inside,

where her power was, Frostpine, Niko, and her friends were silent. They weren't the ones who would be the path for all the magic that was needed here. It was *her* body at risk, not theirs. If she backed off now, they would never hold it against her. Any one of them, in her place, might die of this working, and they all knew it. It was Daja's choice.

She looked again at the caravan. This time she saw the faces of her own family, drowned long months ago. Chandrisa could have been her mother, the ride leader her father. For each adult and child she could name one of the dead: her brother Uneny, always trying to get out of work; mean Aunt Hulweme; Cousin Ziba, who loved to sing. Her little sister, only nine, in her first month aboard ship; her grandmother, seventy-three and toothless, still cooking for their crew.

All that thinking she did in a breath's time. All that memory: it raced through her like a speeding bird.

"Water," she croaked.

Polyam gave her a skin bottle. Daja gulped a few mouthfuls down, then poured the rest over her face and head. She'd never had a chance to save Third Ship Kisubo. Maybe she *couldn't* save Tenth Caravan Idaram—but at least she could try.

She had left her staff in the cart when she'd gone to the head of the caravan. Now she picked it up, running a hand over its smooth brass cap. Leaning on it, she walked into the center of the road and faced the blaze. Its advance on her—on the caravan—had

212

slowed. Some huge trees in its path were refusing to burn, as did the bushes and saplings around them. Magic filled the plants, turning the flames back from bark and leaves.

Rosethorn, she realized. Rosethorn was saving the plants and giving her a chance to think.

The weavings seem to work the best, Niko told her in mind-talk. *This is no time to experiment.*

Despite her fear, Daja had to grin. "When you're right, you're right," she muttered.

No one in the road asked who she was talking to. She looked around: all of them, even Polyam, had retreated. They had left her to face the blaze alone.

What did you expect? she asked herself ironically. Gratitude?

Closing her eyes, she fell into her power's core, plummeting like a dropped hammer. She reached out to gather all she had, pulling it close, shaping it as the right tools for her needs. The others' magic combined with hers as copper and zinc melted to create brass. She swirled Tris and Niko and Briar together, shaping them. To stop this fire, Daja would have to pull it into one great column—there was no time to break it into smaller ones.

I told Rosethorn to ditch the little plants, Briar said matter-of-factly. *She won't give up the trees, though.*

Daja opened her eyes. Here came the fire, roaring between the giant trees like some monster, like an earthquake heard deep underground.

Help me, she thought, not sure if she spoke inside her magic or not.

We are here, replied Niko, Briar, and Tris.

Turning left, Daja reached out one-handed and shoved the onrushing fire toward the strip of road before her. Turning right, she stretched out magic and hand and pushed that side of the wall of flame in. Left again, and push. Right again, and push. Narrower and narrower grew the blaze, leaning toward the middle, thrust by four mages' combined power. At last she could move it no further.

Taking a deep breath, inhaling as much smoke as air and pulling strength from it, Daja flung her arms apart as far as they could go, then swung them back together. The closer her palms got, the more resistance she felt as she squeezed the edges of the blaze together.

Sweat rolled into her eyes, stinging unmercifully. She shook it from her skin and checked both sides one last time, to make sure she had gathered every bit of fire she could. Except for the magic glow in the largest trees, all she saw on either side was charred wood and smoke. Right in front of her roared a tower of fire.

Now she made her power into a gigantic hammer and struck the blaze hard. It flattened. She glimpsed openings between strands of flame.

"Not good enough!" she cried. She struck it again. Something groaned. She didn't dare look away from that huge column of fire to see what was wrong, no matter what. The blaze was too furious; it would break from her grip the moment she got distracted. Again and again she struck, hammering the fire, trying to break it into the many strands she needed to weave it.

I don't feel right, a weak voice said—it belonged to Tris. *I feel . . . loose. Floaty.*

With a bellowed crack, the flame-column broke free of the ground and swayed. It began to rise in the air.

Daja gulped. If it escaped, there was no telling where it would go and what damage it would do.

She raced after it. Seizing its base, she wrapped both arms around it and dragged herself into the column's heart.

Fire was in her ears, her nostrils, her eyes. Her clothes turned to ashes. Her wooden staff vanished; the hot brass cap dropped onto her palm and melted, puddling there. If she screamed then, she never heard it over the monstrous roar. Her grip on Frostpine and Sandry frayed.

Hooks sank into her heart, anchors made of lightning. Tris hung onto Daja, tying herself, Briar, and Niko to the girl, keeping her among the living.

Daja staggered with the fire's weight, and staggered again. It still fought her, trying to rise and break free. Her feet left the ground once, twice.

Where's your root? cried Briar, frantic. *You forgot to*

make a root again! Remember your vine? It needed roots!

Yes! shrieked Tris. *Put a root down, into the rock!*

Why? Daja wondered numbly. She was starting to melt. What had roots to do with anything? *I don't want to.*

Just like a Trader, said Briar scornfully, *always running when things get rough.*

Plague comes to town? That was Tris, a Tris as shrill as a jay. *Traders are the first to leave.*

I lived with them. I know. Sandry's whisper was faint, as if she were dying. *You can't depend on the Tsaw'ha, not ever.*

Daja forced herself to her knees, pushing against the fire's lift. Her knees just barely scraping the road, she dropped forward to press her hands to the earth. Molten brass puddled around her fingers, all that was left of her staff. It stuck her to the dirt like glue.

Stop it, she told her friends. *You only want me angry enough to try putting down a root. You could have just asked.*

She thrust down with all she had.

The earth split. Daja's magic fell into the ground and continued to fall.

Here was rock—hard rock, huge granite slabs jammed together. She found the deep crack formed by two immense pieces, and sent the flames through.

Tris ran past with the fire, pushing it and pulling it along the stone. Niko streaked by to help his student. About to ask what they thought they were doing, Daja took a breath instead and watched. When the flames—when the three mages—erupted into a deep chamber filled with mineral water, she knew what they had in mind. She had been here before.

Dragging more fire with her, she trailed them. Through rock-seams and veins of water they sped as Daja continued to pull her column of flame along. At last the fire itself picked her up and carried her on, racing with its own momentum. Too worn out to resist, she let it drag her until it slammed her into a wall of bitter cold. *That* brought her around.

Mind the glacier, remarked Tris.

Had she eyes, and a face, she would have glared at her friend. *Will this work?* she asked Niko instead. *Can I send it all here?*

Send it, he told her wearily. *It will melt ice for water for Gold Ridge, and there's no risk of creating a volcano with only fire.*

Only fire, he calls it, Daja thought wearily to herself. She turned and swam up her stream—her root?—of flame. Handful by handful, she grabbed at it, sending more through the ground. Finally it screamed past her with all its force, moving on its own. She could let it go, sure now that it would keep going until it smacked the glacier.

With a yell of triumph she exploded from the earth of the road. Back inside her own flesh, she slammed what remained of the flame-pillar into the ground. As soon as most of it was gone, she grabbed the ties that bound Sandry and Frostpine to her and began to reel them in. With them came the fire-scarves they'd been holding at the other end of the caravan. When Daja gripped the weavings, they let go. Into the ground the fire went, crackling ferociously. Daja continued to stuff it down, then all the nearby fires she could get within her power, until she realized that her hands were empty, that they had been empty for some time. She was in the middle of the road on all fours, without a stitch on.

She blinked, and dragged her left hand free of the dirt. Brass coated her palm. It lay in runnels around her fingers and on the back of her hand.

That is going to hurt like *anything* in a bit, she thought, and sat down hard.

For a moment all she could do was cough, and cough, and cough. Finally it occurred to her to look around. The fires were out. All she saw in the forest was burned greenery and thick smoke.

What of the caravan?

She squinted down the road, and choked with dismay. Every human being within her view was on his or her knees in the road, forehead and palms flat on the ground. It was the bow called the Grand Submission, taught to her people centuries ago by some distant emperor. Traders used it only when lives had been saved.

"Get up," she croaked. "I mean it, get up!" I didn't

do it for you, she meant to add, but she was coughing again.

When she got herself under control, one of them crawled forward. To Daja's horror, it was *gilav* Chandrisa, covered in soot, burns all over her clothes and skin. "We know what is owed," the *gilav* said without looking up. "We know what must be paid. What you have done wipes your name from the record of the *trangshi*. We will attest to that and speak for you to the council of our people. You will be *Tsaw'ha* again, and your home will be Tenth Caravan Idaram."

She had not stopped all of the fire. Five people died. Others had lungs damaged by smoke. Rosethorn's burn ointment saw far too much use, among the villagers and among those of the caravan struck by flaming debris. Until their wounded healed, the Traders remained in Gold Ridge.

At least the valley had fresh water. The glacier had produced plenty of it once it was heated by the column of fire, and meltwater still poured into the lake and the wells. In the glacier valley Lady Inoulia ordered work to start on the copper mine, naming it "the Firetamer." Already those who could be spared from repairs were bringing copper and copper ore out of the ground. How much they could get before the snows fell was anyone's guess, but at least Gold Ridge had hope for the spring.

After the first day, Daja knew that her left hand was not hurt as badly as she had feared—it was sore, but only that. It *did* itch, as if the brass were a scab over a healing wound. As the nights got chilly, she found that it ached in the cold. She began to long for the warmth of southern Emelan.

At the very first opportunity, their teachers sat her down to examine her hand. Niko and Frostpine poured spells on the brass, to discover its nature. Nothing seemed to affect it, or to change its mild clasp on her flesh. She *was* able to peel some off, like old skin. More remained, on her palm and the back of her hand, with three strips passing between her fingers to connect them. The metal that she didn't peel away grew back loosely, so she kept pulling off what she could. When she left the peeled-off bits in a metal bowl, they merged like molten brass. If she put a strip of that on her wrist, it lengthened until its ends touched, forming a wristband that she could peel off like wax.

"It *might* go away eventually," Niko said when they could think of nothing else to try on her hand. "I can't say for sure, much as I hate to admit it."

Daja shrugged and tucked the brass-covered hand into her tunic pocket. "At least it doesn't hurt."

On the third day after the fire, Yarrun was buried

in the small castle cemetery. Rosethorn and Briar planted one of the trees that Yarrun had loved so well at the head of his grave.

By the fourth day after the fire, Daja knew that she could use her hand just as she always had. No matter whether she cut up her food, wielded tools, or buttoned her tunics, the brass remained as flexible, and as sensitive, as her own skin. That night she lay awake for a long time, rubbing her metal-covered palm and thinking as hard as she had ever thought in her life.

In the morning, she took all of the brass she had put in the bowl and went to Frostpine with it. They talked long and hard, then called in Niko and talked some more. It was Niko who asked *gilav* Chandrisa to let them borrow the iron vine for a day. Once they had it, they summoned Rosethorn and Briar, and examined the vine inch by inch.

"You'll need a lot of iron for your project," Frostpine told Daja when they took the vine back to the Trader camp. They settled it in Polyam's cart, strapping it in and covering it with blankets.

"I figure twenty rods for the longer parts in the frame—" She stopped, hearing footsteps behind them. They turned to see a group of Traders, each with staff in hand. *Gilav* Chandrisa held two staves: her own, and another. She gave the newer staff to Daja, who ran her fingers over the cap. It was crowned with a many-pointed star of inlaid brass wire—the insignia of

Tenth Caravan Idaram. Two flames, and a sailing ship half-sunk in waves, had been etched into the sides.

"If you are one of us, you require a staff," said the *gilav*. "See that you carry it from now on." She would not look Daja in the face. "When you *do* come to us, we shall see about proper *mimander* training for you."

"It is a good thing you are young," added the *mimander*. "There is time for you to unlearn bad habits, and begin to concentrate your power."

Daja did not like the sound of that. She knew that *mimanders* focused all their attention on mastery of one thing, such as wind or rock. They would make her choose one aspect of her magic and forget the rest.

They would make her give up working with tools.

Of all the Traders standing there, only Polyam met her eyes. She also fell into step with them as Daja and Frostpine walked up the road to the castle.

"They could have been more polite about it," grumbled Daja's teacher.

Polyam chuckled. "Come, come, Master Frostpine. *Tsaw'ha* have a dozen words that mean 'thank you'—each with its drop of dislike. We don't like to *owe*. Our *gilav* won't be happy until the caravan's debt is paid in full."

"Owing me doesn't seem to bother you," Daja pointed out, knowing Polyam was right about thanks and bitterness.

"It does," the Trader replied coolly. "But I know you

223

better than does my mother. I know the prices you paid for what you are. That eases the sting for me—a little, anyway."

Daja worked on her project for an entire month as the weather got colder and the leaves fell. In the end, all of the Winding Circle mages helped her and Frostpine in their forging. Plant and thread magics gave their device the movement and flexibility that iron was not expected to have. Niko guided the placement of interwoven spells, while Tris touched the design with heat, just a drop, to make it as warm as living flesh.

Once the ironwork was done, Daja brought out the large bowl that held all of the liquid brass that she had pulled off her hand in the weeks since the fire. As the others watched, she stretched out small dollops of the stuff as she might pull taffy and draped them over the iron. Once the brass was gone, she let Sandry wrap the finished work in blue silk as she cleaned out the portable forge and returned it to the castle farrier.

That night, after Lark had blown out the candles and left the girls to sleep, Sandry uncovered the spelled lump of crystal that was her night-light. She tossed it from hand to hand for a moment before she asked, "Daja? Have you decided?"

Tris sat up in her own bed, and put on her glasses. "You haven't said a word, and Niko didn't want us bothering you."

Daja realized what they meant. "I didn't know you were worried."

"You should," growled Tris. "You've been carrying that staff everywhere like it's a favorite toy."

"It means a lot to me," Daja said defensively, wishing the redhead didn't always press so hard. "You have no notion."

"You're going with them, then." Sandry's voice was soft. She could have been addressing her pillow, or her night-light.

"No," Daja flatly replied.

The noble's eyes flashed. *"No?"*

Daja sighed. "I could give up our circle, perhaps, or I could give up smithing. I *think* I could, anyway—though I'm not entirely sure. But give up both? I thank you, but no. I've changed too much to go back."

"Why didn't you *say* so before?" Tris demanded, lying back down.

Daja sighed. "I've been thinking about it. All right? May I go to sleep now?"

The next morning Daja was making her bed when Little Bear's hysterical barks and Shriek's answering whistles announced the arrival of guests. Hurriedly she tucked her work under her blanket and went to see what was going on. The newcomers were Traders—Chandrisa, the ride leader, the *mimander*, and Polyam. Knowing why they had come, Daja

225

fetched her new staff and took a seat beside the table, along with her three friends. Lark went for refreshments; Rosethorn summoned Niko and Frostpine. Daja realized that the women also guessed the reason for the Traders' visit.

First, however, there were Trader rituals for serious conversation to be gotten through. Once everyone had a seat, Lark served tea and cakes. The adults chatted about the aftermath of the fire as they politely sipped and ate. The four young people fed their cakes to the dog on the sly and tried to be patient.

Finally *gilav* Chandrisa put down her cup, and folded her hands in her lap. "We take the road at dawn," she said flatly.

"The snows will begin in six days," added the *mimander*, invisible behind his lemon-colored veils. No one questioned his certainty—*mimanders* often specialized in weather magic of some kind.

"You must pack and be in Polyam's cart at first light," the *gilav* told Daja. "Do not hold up our departure."

Daja picked up her staff with both hands. "I thank you, but I cannot accept this." Getting to her feet, she offered the staff to Chandrisa. "I've been a *lugsha* for too long. I cannot give that up." She swallowed hard. Even knowing her answer hadn't prepared her for how difficult it was to actually *say* the words. "I cannot give up my new home, and my new family. I would be grateful if you just took my name from the

226

record of *trangshi*. That way I can do business with the *Tsaw'ha*, without anyone being *qunsuanen*."

Chandrisa looked at the staff and at Daja. "Our debt will be paid in full? You will not hold us owing?"

"Once I am no longer *trangshi*, we will be even," Daja said. Taking a step closer to Chandrisa, she offered the staff again.

The *gilav* wrapped brown fingers around the wood, then let go. "Keep the staff, as a sign of friendship," she said drily. "As a promise that we shall do business together. I hope it will please you when I say that our messenger went south two weeks ago, to correct the records of your name."

Daja leaned the staff on her chair, biting her lip so as not to cry. She cleared her throat. "Tenth Caravan Idaram and I are clear, but there is another matter. I owe a personal debt, and I must pay it."

Briar and Tris knew what she meant. They went into the girls' bedroom and returned with her creation, still in its blue silk wrapping.

Daja turned to Polyam. "If not for you, I never would have had a chance to wipe my name from the *trangshi* book." Taking her work from Briar, she carried it over to Polyam's chair. "This is actually from all of us," she told the woman quietly as Sandry pulled the silk wrappings away. Polyam's jaw dropped; Chandrisa and the two male Traders leaned forward, intent.

It was a metal leg, shaped entirely of thin iron rods and joints. Everything was covered in a gleaming brass skin. Briar tickled the metal sole. It twitched, just as a living foot might twitch. Tris laid a hand on the shin, and the knee bent.

Polyam stretched out a hand that shook violently and touched the leg. She yanked her fingers away, shocked. "It's *warm!*"

"It should act just as a real limb would," Niko said. "We tested it enough. And you have the rest of today to try it out."

"It will shape itself to your flesh," explained Frostpine.

"You'll be able to take it off whenever you like," Sandry put in.

"You can even bathe with it," added Briar.

It was Tris who asked the question on everyone's mind: "Do you want to try it on?"

The room was absolutely silent. Even the dog sat quietly, his dark eyes on Polyam. Only Shriek moved, picking up crumbs from the table.

At last Polyam nodded.

Rosethorn and Lark helped her to remove her wooden peg and roll her legging up to bare what remained of her thigh. Gently Frostpine and Daja slid the open sleeve at the top of their creation over Polyam's stump, placing the leg so it matched the angle of her good leg. As they settled it, Frostpine showed her the brads to press on the uppermost rim of the metal, so it would relax enough for her to take it off or to put it back on.

Once the leg was settled, Polyam gasped as brass-coated iron shifted, molding itself to her flesh. "It lives!"

Daja watched the metal adjust, frowning absent-mindedly. All her power was bent on her work as it fit itself to Polyam. "It's supposed to," she murmured.

The metal leg stiffened, then bent. "Work it as you might a real leg," Frostpine urged.

The metal foot twitched. Very slowly the toes wriggled. Polyam braced her thigh with her hands, extended the metal limb, then pointed her foot.

"Try standing," suggested Daja.

They had to assist her: she didn't seem to remember how to move with two good legs. Finally she was able to walk around the room and out onto the balcony alone.

"It shouldn't chafe," Rosethorn called to her. "It's entirely covered with the brass skin. Daja will tell you, hers doesn't irritate her flesh at all."

Polyam lifted her real leg onto the balcony rail, balancing entirely on her new limb. When she looked back at Daja, the girl held up her left hand and twiddled her fingers. The gold-colored brass glinted. "It's like it really *is* skin," Daja explained. "That's what gave me the idea."

Rosethorn took a jar of ointment out to Polyam. "If it *does* chafe, this should help. Just rub it wherever you have trouble."

"Keep the limb clean," Frostpine added. "It can be

washed, but I suggest a drop or two of oil in the foot joints every week, and a palmful into the knee."

Polyam ran a hand over the metal encasing her thigh, then put both feet on the ground once more. No one mentioned that her good eye streamed tears. "I could wear *clothes* again," she whispered.

"Even boots," Lark suggested with a smile.

"You can ride," was Sandry's contribution. "If you want, that is."

"We tried to think of everything," said Niko. "I hope you'll keep in touch and let us know how you fare."

"If problems arise, send word to Winding Circle. We'll come to you," added Frostpine. "But—I don't believe you will have problems."

Polyam wiped her face on her sleeve, then turned to Daja. "This is more than payment—"

"No," Daja interrupted. "You gave me the chance to clear my name. Now we don't owe each other a thing." Looking at the carpet, she added softly, "I *would* like to be friends."

Rough arms swept her up in a hug. "We are friends," Polyam assured her in a fierce whisper. "We will *always* be friends."

The next day the mages roused themselves at dawn and joined the duke and Lady Inoulia in seeing Tenth Caravan Idaram off. It made Daja breathless to see

Polyam, in trousers and boots, swing into the saddle of a brown gelding as the ride leader signaled for the caravan to move out. Polyam followed him with the other riders, half-turned in the saddle so that she could wave, until the turn of the road hid her from sight.

Frostpine slung an arm around Daja's shoulders. "Even if you never made another thing, the Traders will sing your name for generations," he said cheerfully. "Of course, you're going to make plenty more things."

"I am?" she asked, looking up into his laughing eyes.

"Yes indeed—starting with nails." He ignored Daja's groan. "I believe you've made only a single bucketful the whole time we've been here, and I need a way to measure how much you've changed since our arrival. Nails will serve that need quite well."

"Can they wait?" asked the duke, soft-voiced. "If the snows fall in five days, I would like to go myself—tomorrow."

"Home," said Lark with a happy sigh. "That sounds *wonderful.*"

"I'll make nails all winter, if I can just do them at home," Daja told Frostpine.

He sighed. "Oh, all right. We can make nails as well at Winding Circle as we can here."

"Better," Tris muttered to Daja. "At least at home

it's warm." Her breath steamed in the icy mountain air.

Daja grinned. Not only would they be warmer, but they would be near the sea again. "Last one to the rooms gets to do all the packing!" she cried, and ran for the castle.